TRADE WINDS
OF THE
HEART

A Romance Novel

by

KRYSTINA POWELLS

KP BOOKS

Book Layout ©2017 BookDesignTemplates.com

1. FIC027020 Romance/Contemporary—Fiction, 2. FIC044000 Women—Fiction, 3. FIC027260 Romance/African American-Fiction

Trade Winds of the Heart/Krystina Powells-- 1st ed.

ISBN 978-976-96500-0-8 Paperback
ISBN 978-976-96500-1-5 Ebook
ISBN 978-976-96500-2-2 Kindle

Dedication:
I am grateful for the undying support of my loving husband who always pushes me to be the best that I can be. Many thanks to my parents who instilled in me the value of appreciating the Creator, the importance of loving life, and the determination to fulfill my dreams. Special thanks to my brother, sisters and constructive critics. Heartfelt thanks to my editors, book marketer, and dear friends. Most of all, I thank the Most High for His wise principles that guide me every day of my life.

FOREWORD

The **trade winds** are the dominant pattern of eastbound surface winds found in the tropics. These steady winds allowed colonial development into the Americas and led trade routes to become set up across the Atlantic and Pacific oceans. During the Age of Sail, this system of prevailing winds made various points of the planet easy or difficult to approach.

CHAPTER 1

The holiday season with all of its festivities, celebrating the end of one year and the beginning of another, was finally over. Pumpa had won the Carnival Road March as everyone had expected, and for weeks, his song "Back Together" blared at every beach bash, house party, and family gathering.

Sadly, the customary, year-end hype was slowly petering out, and reality was quickly setting in. Still, the islanders were thankful that St. Croix was finally enjoying the reprieve they had craved from the usually hot and humid Caribbean weather.

The trade winds were making their rounds, but about this time of the year, more fiercely. They swirled violently around a cluster of dingy, brown buildings a few miles from the western coast, and the shaky aluminum louvers of a small, two-bedroom apartment rattled with every gusty encounter.

Unstirred, Kayla Jackson, stared blankly at the newspaper spread out in front of her on the small, well-worn wooden dining table. Her hair was wrapped in a silk madras head tie, her head was bowed as if in prayer, and her eyes peeled in anticipation of something-- anything. She was looking at the Want Ads in the *St. Croix Avis Newspaper*. At twenty-four years old with two children, there was no doubt that a job was a priority for Kayla. The black and white print was goggling back at her silently, sending the message that this was serious business.

Kayla remembered when she was seven years old, the day she saw people erecting the sign with the new name for these build- ings--The Walter I.M. Hodge Pavilion. There was a ceremony with the Governor and everyone else who liked to be on television. Some probably wishing the news would find its way to the White House, in hopes that President Clinton might get a sneak peek of the great things that were happening on this small, seemingly in- significant island.

"What's a pavilion?" she looked up and asked her mother.

"Look it up in the dictionary," her mother said, hurrying along paying no attention to all the commotion they had just passed.

pa·vil·ion

pə ˈvilyən/

noun

    1. *a building or similar structure used for a specific purpose, in particular.*

    2. *a usually highly decorated projecting subdivision of a building.*

Kayla looked up from the dictionary and gazed out of the apart- ment window. She scanned the dingy community where she had lived all the seven years of her life. She saw the ugly, depressing brown colored buildings, guys sitting on the steps smoking, kids riding their bikes on the sidewalk. She studied the mothers coming home from work, screaming at their kids, laughing with their friends, and greeting elderly neighbors--all at the same time. I guess we live in a "structure used for a specific purpose," because this place ain't "highly decorated", she concluded.

Kayla was in no mood to look out of the window seventeen years later. There was no need for confirmation. Nothing much had changed. *Anyway, I need a job; that's for sure.* Kayla's two eager eyes continued surveying the page full of ads with words like *looking for, needed,* and *wanted.* She was sure to read each carefully, but her mind wandered again.

Omari thinks that sitting outside on those funky steps every day, trying to sell drugs to the same strung-out people is going to make him a superstar. I'm still waiting for all the things he promised me when we were in high school. We all still live here in the Walter I.M. Hodge Pavilion deep in the heart of Frederiksted, behind God's back. She silently blasted her children's father.

Kayla's mother, Margo, was the one person who always believed in her. When Kayla became pregnant in her last year of high school with her daughter, Samaria, she could feel her mother's disappointment.

"Kayla, you have so much potential. Why you went and mess yourself up with that bwoy?" Margo said with tears in her eyes.

Omari Smith and his mother, on the other hand, had disagreed. "Ms. Margo keeping her children so prim and proper like they better than all a we," Omari's mother told him one day.

Both were well aware that Kayla was certainly different from all of the other girls in the neighborhood. Besides being pretty, she was a brilliant student. In spite of that, Omari was bent on proving Margo wrong.

"They gon see. Kayla gon be my gyul forever," he promised his mother.

The other neighbors were convinced that Omari would never get with Kayla, and he resented that. With one child on the way, he was on the verge of surprising them all.

Once Kayla became pregnant the second time with her son, Adjoni, she was convinced that her mother had given up on her for sure. She didn't even have the courage to announce that she had missed her period. Mothers figure out those things eventually, she was sure.

Her mother did work it out, but all she said to her daughter was, "You ain't look right, Kayla." It was hard for Kayla to forget her mother's voice that day. It was low and tense.

The two actually never spoke about it. Margo supported as she always did, while Omari left Kayla hanging with two kids that he had no means of providing for. Kayla knew she had crushed her mother more than the people who discriminated against them for living in this pavilion. Her mother had endured so many injustices but always carried herself with such dignity.

"Find anything yet?" her mother asked, sticking her head out between the overhead cabinets and the kitchen counter. The newspaper her daughter was mulling over on the dining table appeared in clear view.

Kayla was jolted from her thoughts. "Mommy, I know I need a job, but St. Croix is a small place. How much jobs you think out there for me to choose from? My options are limited."

"Well, keep tryin', child," Margo said as she passed the dining table and strolled back into her room to get the watch she had left on her dresser.

"That's what I'm doing, Ma."

"You can't keep relying on Omari's lazy behind to throw you some change for the kids whenever he remembers," Margo said loud and clear as she walked down the short hallway towards her room.

"You spelled that out a hundred times already, Mommy. But I hate looking for jobs. I feel so self-conscious and vulnerable, like a puppy in the window of a pet shop jumping feverishly, barking, 'Take me, take me!'"

Kayla sucked her teeth softly, careful not to let her mother hear her frustration which might be interpreted as disrespect. She knew that the distinct sound imitating slurping up liquid through a straw while clenching teeth irritated Caribbean parents. There was no doubt that the tendentious old habit of sucking teeth was viewed as rude and immodest to the older generation only when the younger generation subconsciously followed the tradition. The irony made Kayla chuckle to herself. "Besides, the jobs that make sense only go to certain people," she continued.

Margo eyed Kayla as she passed the table again and headed to the front door. She half-smiled. There was a latent pain she felt for her daughter, but as a mother, she had to be tough. "I got to go to work, but don't give up. Love ain't going to pay these bills."

Margo worked as a housekeeper at one of the villas in East End owned by a Jewish family. The Benhams treated Margo well. In fact, in the summer the Benhams would let her children, Kayla and Malik (Mally), use the pool while she worked. It was fun for them. It didn't feel like the Benhams discriminated against her family at all. "Not all white people are the same," she would tell her children.

The Benhams had a son wind daughter too--Michael and Elena. Kayla had always told Margo that she suspected that Elena and Mally had a thing for each other. Neither of them admitted it, but

Kayla said she could tell. Michael was way older than the other three which meant that he had saved them from drowning many times. Margo always remembers Michael calling her daughter "Cute Kayla". Deep down inside she felt that Kayla knew he meant it.

Margo opened the front door and sighed.

Sucking her teeth softly and rolling her eyes at the paper in front of her, Kayla refused to look up at her mother standing in the doorway. She sensed the blinding glare from the morning sun landing on her mother's full figure.

"It's a total waste of time. One look at me and 'Not you!' is written all over their faces. No matter how hard I try to impress, ain't even make sense," she lamented quietly.

"Well, do what the teachers say in school, in your business class--no chewing gum, keep your hands on your lap, watch the people in the face."

"You mean 'eye contact'? Yes, I do all of that, Mommy. I can't figure out what I doing wrong," she said. "Maybe deep down inside I already know," she exhaled.

Scanning the first column on the page, Kayla found a position that there was no doubt she could fill: "Mc Islands Burgers Looking for Entry Level Staff".

Kayla knew tons of people who worked at McIsland's Burgers. *It's the employer of choice for people living in pavilions,* Kayla thought. *Which should not be surprising since Mac I's is our fast food restaurant of choice,* she admitted. Kayla figured it was a symbiotic relationship of sorts like she had learned in Mr. Matthew's science class.

But what type of symbiosis?

She wasn't sure. Was it mutualism, where both sides benefited from the relationship; commensalism, when only one side benefits and the other side remains unaffected; or parasitism, when one side benefits and the other side suffers. Kayla was sure that the jury was still out on this.

Though some of her neighbors had worked their way up from entry-level staff to managers, it only meant that they got to bring home more stale food.

Working at a burger joint was definitely out of the question. Kayla wanted something that had growth potential. It was not that she had anything against any of the world's great fast-food restaurant chains. They were actually the only restaurants she could afford, and she took her kids to eat at some of them once in a while as a treat. It's just that Kayla couldn't see herself reaching very far if all she was doing was flipping burgers and filling up cardboard containers with french fries.

Kayla could sense that the winds were creating an undercurrent in her neighborhood, and she was desperately trying to buck the tide. She concluded that it would be hard to break the cycle if she even considered employment at a burger joint, albeit gainful. "My children need me to move on," she whispered. In their eyes Kayla saw an innocent optimism about life; they were always dreaming. *But there is a cruel world waiting to meet them,* she thought. *One intent on crushing their hopes and dreams. It will smile at them and then devilishly say to them, "Thank you so much for coming" while knowing full well that there was no chance whatsoever.*

"OK, so back to job hunting," Kayla said, moaning softly as she continued reading each ad. There were tons of babysitting jobs. I ain't sleeping over at nobody's house, leaving my kids behind like a wet nurse in slavery days, she brooded.

Most ads asking for "Babysitters" were for parents who wanted a night out without their kids so that they could hang out with friends and enjoy some adult conversation. Or they just fancied eating at a restaurant without the hassle of requesting a high chair, rationalizing a tantrum (which usually includes the throwing of food), or enduring some other type of indignity that children have a knack for putting their parents through in public. In that case, it would be best to stay home or just go to a drive-through. Then again, sometimes parents were simply looking for babysitters so that they could attend "Adult Only" functions.

The bottom line was that most of these ads requiring a babysitter were for the nighttime.

All Kayla could see was a long list of jobs that she knew would make her depressed and dread waking up for work in the morning. Did she want to work in an office, in a restaurant or with children? At this point, Kayla really didn't know what she wanted to do, but she did know that she had better find a job. Her mother didn't mind helping her and the kids, but like she said this morning for the millionth time "love don't pay the bills." Kayla got the point.

At the bottom of the third column, Kayla spotted a prospect.

"JFL Hospital looking for Cook staff and Kitchen Assistant. Please apply in person. Contact: Mrs. Judy Merchant"

I can apply for this one. Kayla highlighted the spot in yellow. "How much experience do I need to help cook? I cook all the time. My kids love my food," she muttered as she drew a red circle around the blurb. At least this job wouldn't be at a fast food joint.

Kayla settled on going to see Mrs. Merchant. If everything turned out right, she would get a chance to prove herself. Not only that, Merchant sounded like a black, local name. Kayla twinkled. That simple, little label made her feel hopeful.

CHAPTER 2

The next day, when Kayla walked out of her building, she looked around and took a deep breath. The air was crisp and clean, the sky, clear and bright. It was as if each building had its own special ray of sunlight.

The sun really shines on the good and the bad, Kayla mused. That is so beautiful. Thank God for that. Everyone has a chance to start a new day. I hope this is a new day for me.

But the brightness diminished as soon as she headed towards the crusty steps outside the building. Just glimpsing the crowded steps made Kayla feel deceived by the refreshing morning air and the glorious sunshine. Every square inch of the steps was crowded with guys who did not want to look for a real job but found time to congregate outside every day in exactly the same spot.

"Hey baby, weh you going?" Omari asked as Kayla maneuvered her way down the crowded steps.

Kayla grimaced and glared at her children's father. "I ain't your baby, that's number one. And to look for a job, number two. You know your children need to eat, right?" Kayla sucked her teeth loudly.

"Why you gotta be like that?" Omari's voice was thin and squeaky; his face rosy and boyish, exposing his shame--his babies' mama had just outed him in front of his boys.

"Like how--concerned?" Kayla was tired of waiting for financial support from this dude.

A real waste.

Kayla made it to the bottom of the steps and cringed. She knew that Omari was eyeing her, and she had no intention of returning the favor.

As she moved along, Building 4 which housed the administrative office came into view. Kayla took a deep breath. She often wondered if Ms. Bishop, the manager, had anything to do with the way the Pavilion was designed. Everyone coming and going had to pass by this one building. She was sure that Ms. Bishop was, by far, the nosiest person on earth.

Actually, Kayla seriously contemplated squeezing through a hole in the chain link fence that some boys had cut out probably in an attempt to avoid passing by the office themselves. But the truth was that Kayla had nothing to hide. She was going out. She didn't need to give an explanation. Certainly not to Ms. Bishop. Also, Kayla didn't want to risk ripping her clothes on the way to this interview.

Arlina Bishop was in her late fifties, very thin and always wore her glasses halfway down her nose. Her slight stateside accent was from her early years as a child growing up in Saint Paul, Minnesota with her aunt. She had come back to live in St. Croix with her mother when she was in her late teens.

She had worked in the office of the Walter I.M. Hodge Pavilion for over twenty years and had seen a lot of kids grow up there; including Kayla and her brother, Malik. Some had moved on and out of this pavilion, but most were like stranded sailors on a deserted island. Kayla, on the other hand, wanted to be like the captain of a sailing ship choosing her own course to follow.

"You look sharp today, Kayla," Ms. Bishop said as Kayla walked passed, examining the young lady's outfit carefully.

The rasping, humorless voice and its owner had been a constant irritant to Kayla for many years. She suspected that Ms. Bishop had to be using binoculars, because Kayla could never figure out how the woman knew when she was coming.

Kayla had learned the drill, yet her brain could never work fast enough to formulate an answer that was good enough to prevent another question from spewing out of the manager's mouth. "Yes" was the best Kayla could come up with at the moment.

"A job. I hope. Because that boy ain't going to help you and your kids get anywhere." The stern farrowed face stared Kayla down as if it were of a prophetess.

"OK, Ms. Bishop," Kayla said. She was itching to say a lot more, but she had no time for the crosstalk. Kayla was on her way to look for a job. She could let it all out in her mind as she foot it up the long road to catch the bus.

As Kayla walked away, she could feel Ms. Bishop's eyes piercing holes in her back, but she preferred not to know what was going through the manager's mind.

Does every conversation with this woman need to be the same? Kayla thought.

The playback was unreal.

"How do pretty, smart girls like you end up with bums like those?" Ms. Bishop would often press, pushing for an explanation and glancing at the steps. Her voice dry and unsolicited.

"Things happen, Ms. Bishop."

"Can't you learn from the mistakes of others?" Ms. Bishop would insist, trying to understand.

"We just get caught up," Kayla would say, knowing that Ms. Bishop would never understand.

The truth was that Kayla herself did not fully understand how her life had spun out of control, and why it seemed to be heading downward into a smelly drain leading to emptiness.

That was the irksome conversation Kayla was expecting this morning. Fortunately, Ms. Bishop was too busy arguing with the gardener about the weeds in front of her building to address that issue with her tenant for the hundredth time. Her questions were the same, and Kayla's answers didn't change much either. The customary performance was saved for yet another day.

As Kayla marched up the straight road to catch a bus, Omari's story rolled over in her head. She stared at the full-grown, tropical almond tree in the distance. There were no blossoms as yet, just huge leaves and thick branches waiting patiently for their flowery companions. The inconspicuous blossoms would appear in a few months, and soon after, the school kids would raid the tree long before Kayla could get a taste of the fruit.

"Greedy kids," she muttered.

The tree was a constant reminder of where Kayla was in her journey and her life--midway up the endlessly boring road.

As she stepped over the tree's large, aggressive fibrous roots that cracked up the dirty, concrete sidewalk, she thought about obstacles--like Omari.

His story was a short, sad one--much like mine is turning out to be, Kayla thought. His father had left, and his mother had grown distracted with trying to find another man. Omari was a smart guy who just couldn't navigate his way through the sea of emotional baggage. His drug-dealing uncle and cousins had filled in the gaps along the way. The odds had been stacked against him from the start.

As hard as it was for Kayla to look at her children's father wasting his tragic life away, she still wanted Samaria and Adjoni to have a relationship with him. Knowing this hapless father was better than knowing no father at all, she felt. After all, Kayla had her own pathetic version of a father--Kenrick. Although Omari and Kayla eventually went separate ways, she still endured his childishness for the sake of their kids. In the meantime, he had another clueless girl very pregnant with his third child.

Kayla ended her sojourn to the top of the road arriving at the gas station on the corner. She chose to take a bus that was empty enough to find a good seat and full enough to prevent the driver from trying to pick up every person he thought he saw. Kayla estimated that the bus ride would take about thirty minutes as long as most of the passengers were going as far as she was, or further.

On almost every bus ride there was someone who wanted to sit closer to her than they needed to. This ride was no different.

"How much closer you want me to get to the window?" Kayla asked the guy who was brushing up on her.

"Ah right," he said as he eyed her with a funny grin plastered on his face. He then eased up about an inch.

With a little more elbow room Kayla could look out of the window comfortably and think about the next move in her life. There were buildings and cars and people and trees--lots of trees. Everything flew by too quickly to focus on any one thing. This scene was a fitting metaphor for her life. Her life was full of drama--different actors, scenery and props, but absolutely no plot.

"Right here!" Kayla shouted from the back of the bus as she saw her stop coming up.

The bus driver pulled over, Kayla handed him his two dollars and got out. As she got closer to the entrance of the hospital, many thoughts flooded her mind. The place hadn't changed much since she was there five years ago for the birth of her son. The food probably hadn't changed much either, she supposed. "But who expects gourmet dishes from a hospital," she chuckled to herself.

Instantly, her mind shifted to the quandary she was in. The government was no longer supporting her, and her mother had made it clear that she was following suit. Plus, Kayla didn't enjoy begging for handouts. She had done everything in her power to make this mission a success. She had spent all night trying to find the right outfit to wear. She stationed herself in front of the mirror practicing how to speak during the interview, and she prayed fervently that she would get this job. In reality, she had already faced a few obstacles on her way here early this morning.

In spite of it all, Kayla was trying to keep a steady pace.

With every step closer to her goal Kayla reviewed her prior work experience. The last job she'd had was at Paradise Mart during the busy Christmas shopping season. It had been clear that professionalism wasn't a requirement in that place. Before that, she'd worked for the summer through an on-the-job training program sponsored by the government which focused on helping underprivileged youths. That summer she'd been assigned to work in a government office.

Kayla was still not sure what type of service the office actually provided, and hadn't thought the workers had known either--nor had they cared. A paycheck every other Thursday was the point. Of course, no one dared to miss work on that day. That was the day they all provided the service they were supposed to--whatever that was.

"The cafeteria is to your left, through those double doors." Those were the simple instructions from the lady at the front desk that jerked Kayla back to reality.

"Now, to find Mrs. Merchant and try to land this job," Kayla said to herself.

She pushed open the two large, gray double-acting hinged doors to the cafeteria which revealed a clean, uncomplicated space. There were large glass windows that made the cafeteria feel light and airy. Small, round aluminum tables paired with blue, plastic stackable bucket chairs were scattered about with no real order, and there was a stainless steel serving station with two busy employees. They both stopped what they were doing and looked warily at Kayla as she wandered in. The two pairs of eyes followed her as she advanced towards them.

"Good morning. I am here to see Mrs. Merchant," Kayla said without a pause and swallowed softly trying not to appear nervous. She then grinned at the woman staring her down from behind the serving station.

"Merchie, someone here to you," the female worker announced to her boss, refusing to make eye contact again with the lady standing in front of her. "How much people going to apply for this one job?" she said under her breath to the other worker who was standing next to her. They both chuckled and decided to study Kayla once more from head to toe.

The female worker was a black girl with large box braids and a sour face. She was standing next to a heavy-set Hispanic guy whose face was broad and humorless. Kayla thought that perhaps they must be quite annoyed at the parade of eager applicants. She eyed them discreetly and wondered if they were both from a pavilion, like herself. *This episode has Mc Islands Burgers' junk food written all over it.* Kayla flinched.

There were, obviously, quite a few hopeful applicants. Kayla knew she couldn't have been the only individual interested in a job that had been advertised in the Wanted Ads of a local newspaper that was read by most people on the island, many of whom were unemployed like she was. Jokes aside, she was secretly hoping that would be the case. *The less competition, the better.*

When Kayla looked at her life now, it was so different from what she had imagined it would have been. She used to be confident and sure of herself. Now, she always felt defeated. Where she'd lived, who her family was, or what they had were never hurdles for her. She'd done exceptionally well in school and had been consistently on the Honor Roll. Her teachers had always boasted about her grades, as if they'd been responsible for her intelligence.

So what had happened? Omari? Having children too early? Which of the two--or both? She really didn't know or maybe she was afraid of the answer. Was she her own worst enemy? She was a twenty-four-year-old single mother of two, but that might not be the reason either, she concluded. "Now ain't the time to find yourself, girl," she said to herself. "You need this job bad. So focus!"

"Hi, I'm Mrs. Merchant," said the sweet, white face that appeared.

It was hard to miss the strong stateside accent. Kayla winced. This was not going the way she had envisioned. With a name like "Merchant", this woman was supposed to be at least black, if not local.

"Nice to meet you. How may I help you?" Mrs. Merchant continued.

Kayla was face to face with Judy Merchant, a white lady in her late forties and very attractive. The lady was well-dressed and had her hair pulled away from her face in a slick ponytail. If Kayla had seen her on the street, she would never have placed Mrs. Merchant in hospital administration. Real estate or design, maybe; but not a hospital. She obviously had to have lived in St. Croix for a considerable amount of time and had a good enough rapport with the staff to be affectionately called "Merchie". Kayla knew that Crucians weren't accustomed to getting too familiar with foreigners too fast.

Kayla cleared her throat to change accents. It would be unthinkable for her to use raw Crucian dialect during an interview; definitely not with a non-local like Mrs. Merchant.

"Good Morning, Mrs. Merchant. My name is Kayla Jackson. I saw the ad in the newspaper for a Cook Staff and Kitchen Assistant," Kayla articulated as best she could, eliminating any pauses which meant that the interviewer could not reject her early on. She was, however, already feeling doubtful.

"Let me have you fill out an application," Mrs. Merchant said and left to retrieve the required paperwork.

Typical. Applications. Kayla despised them. On the other hand, at least it meant that there was still an opening for her.

Mrs. Merchant returned with a one-leaf application form that was printed on both sides. "You can sit over there." She pointed to one of the small metal tables with four blue chairs. "When you're finished, we can talk a little bit more about the position." Her voice was calm and toneless.

"OK," Kayla said and fake-smiled. She sat down pensively, took a deep breath and examined the application.

If all goes well, it wouldn't be like the Scholastic Aptitude Test I took in the twelfth grade, she thought.

The last time Kayla had filled out a job application, she felt as if it would have been graded. It goes without saying that was one of the instances when she did not get the job.

Name: ______________. This was easy for Kayla. *At least I know this,* she thought.

Male []　Female []. Kayla wondered, *Does my gender make a differ-ence? Anyway, it's clear which box I would be checking.*

Prior Work Experience:

This one made Kayla stop and think. *Should I include my Paradise Mart stint and the government summer job? If I omitted those two, I probably wouldn't have much to disclose.* Kayla rolled her eyes. Bridging the gap between joblessness and gainful employment was a real hassle. She settled on including the small-time gigs. Anything was better than nothing, she felt.

Education:

High school for sure! Kayla was elated that she could confi-dently circle the number 12, thanks to her mother.

College/University:

There was a pause. Kayla inhaled and held her breath for a few seconds. This section always made her feel uneasy. It was as if the words were reading her mind. It was always a time for reflection.

Would she ever be able to fill in these lines one day? A lot of her schoolmates had already gone off to college and gotten their degrees while Kayla was home busy breastfeeding and changing diapers.

"Finished?" Mrs. Merchant appeared again.

Kayla jumped inside. "Yes, I am," she replied.

"So what made you decide to apply for this job?" Mrs. Merchant asked curiously (tired of the applicants who wasted her time).

Kayla wanted to choose her words carefully. Sure, she could be brutally honest and say, "Because I need a job." And then ramble on and on about her children's father not pulling his weight. She could go even further with her spiel and tell about how distressing it is to always have to ask her already strapped mother for money. But then she wouldn't sound like someone who really wanted to work and learn. It would most likely go over as if she just needed the money, which was actually the main reason she was applying for this job in the first place. She had to come up with a convincing answer. "I'm looking for a position that will offer an opportunity for me to learn and grow," she said in a clear, low voice.

"Interesting," Mrs. Merchant said, impressed by the response.

Yes, I know, very interesting, Kayla thought. *Good answer. No more questions please. Just give me the job, train me and then I can expect a check in the next three weeks.* She smiled at her interviewer.

"This position is entry-level and involves a lot of prepping. Do you cook?" Mrs. Merchant asked as her eyes reviewed Kayla's responses on the form. She looked up again waiting for an answer.

Kayla cleared her throat. "Every day," she said without explaining that she had two hungry mouths to feed every single day. She chose to leave her children out of this dialogue. The job had yet to become hers. Revealing those two little details would clearly be too much information (TMI) at this point.

"OK. It will also require working with a nutritionist and, at some point, maybe even delivering food to our patients." Mrs. Merchant decided that getting all of that out from the get-go was necessary to weed out the duds.

"I look forward to being trained," Kayla said, hoping that Mrs. Merchant would sense a desire to learn and not desperation.

"No college or university education, huh?" Mrs. Merchant twitched her nose as if it were a concern.

Kayla picked up on the expression on her interviewer's face. "No, not yet. It is something I am seriously considering, though." *Good answer.* She was on a roll.

"What would you like to study?" asked Mrs. Merchant.

Think, think....think. In elementary school, Kayla had signed out a book from the library about how Florence Nightingale had revolutionized the world of medicine with her reforms in the organization and administration of hospitals. Ever since then, nursing had intrigued her. She wanted to become a nurse. There was a Licensed Practical Nurse certificate program at the University of the Virgin Islands, but it always seemed out of her reach. Motherhood was complicated. Perhaps, with the kids now both in school, one day it might be a real possibility. "I am seriously thinking about doing the Licensed Practical Nurse course at UVI," Kayla said as earnestly as she could.

"So you know about that certification program? Good choice. Do you know it is also offered here at the hospital to our staff?" Mrs. Merchant was pleased that at least this applicant had something to say that made sense.

"Really?" Kayla opened her eyes wide with surprise.

"It is good to have goals. Don't ever stop trying to achieve more in life."

Kayla questioned whether Mrs. Merchant had the same conversation with all of the applicants? Did she have it with the duo over there behind the counter serving food? It would be interesting if they were taking the course too or was it that Mrs. Merchant saw something positive in Kayla? Kayla couldn't tell, but she did know that she liked the way this interview was going. Someone else was willing to challenge her. Kayla had the chance to be more than another young, single mother from the ghetto.

"Do you have staff here taking the course?" Kayla was burning to find out.

Looking over at the two workers at the serving station and then looking back at Kayla, Mrs. Merchant said, "The tragedy of life doesn't lie in not reaching your goal. The tragedy lies in having no goal to reach."

"Benjamin Mays!" said Kayla.

"You know about him?" Mrs. Merchant asked.

"I did a report on him and other civil rights leaders for Black History Month." Kayla gazed at her interviewer with pride.

"Great! So, when can you start?" Mrs. Merchant stood up. She had made her choice.

Finally, a keeper.

"When would you like for me to start?" Kayla asked, smiling while biting her lips.

"If you don't have any arrangements to make, you can start tomorrow morning at eight o'clock."

"I can start tomorrow."

"We have uniforms here in different sizes. When you come tomorrow, we'll talk some more about that. You'll have to go to Human Resources to fill out some more forms. I'll call them to let them know you will be coming in. That should give them some time to prepare the paperwork for you. It was nice meeting you, Ms. Jackson. I look forward to working with you. See you tomorrow." Mrs. Merchant's face gleamed. She had finally met an applicant who had promise.

"It was nice meeting you too, Mrs. Merchant. I look forward to working with you." Kayla stood up with one hand gripping the metal table.

"Merchie, phone for you," interrupted the Hispanic guy, apparently sensing his boss' special interest in this new applicant. (The two had spent more than the usual ten minutes that Mrs. Merchant allotted to sift out the lemons.)

"We have to talk more about the LPN certification course," Mrs. Merchant said gleaming as she waved her index finger in the air and scurried away.

"I would love that," Kayla said grinning from ear to ear. She managed to pry herself from the table and eased out of the cafeteria.

"I hope this one can live up to Merchie's expectations," the guy whispered to his co-worker as they watched Kayla exit their turf.

"I know. Merchie ain't easy," the female worker said under her breath.

"With those looks, I give her two weeks--like the last one," he said and smirked. The two employees eyed each other and giggled.

As Kayla hurried down the long road away from the hospital, she looked up at the clear, blue Caribbean sky. This was the start of a new day for her. She felt like hopping away in an imaginary game of hopscotch. Her face broke into a sunny, childlike smile. It was an involuntary action really. She covered her smile and looked over self-consciously at the white guy driving a big shiny blue truck heading in the direction of the hospital. He had stopped to allow a brown speckled hen and her chicks cross the street. The driver's face wasn't clear, and Kayla could barely see his eyes. But, she was sure that they were full of compassion.

A line had formed behind the truck as the fussy mother hen and her clutch of chicks took their sweet time strolling across the busy street. Kayla wanted to call out to the driver and thank him for giving the little family a chance. They deserved a new day too.

Kayla was beside herself rehearsing over and over in her mind what she would say if someone asked her where she was working.

"So what are you doing for yourself?" That would be the inquiry.

I'm working at the hospital.

Hospital! There would be amazement.

Yes, the hospital, she would reply proudly.

Kayla had nothing planned past that point in the conversation. The dialogue would end abruptly before getting into the details like, "So where in the hospital?" A hospital kitchen isn't exactly a dream job. A job, yes. But definitely not a dream job.

As Kayla walked past the Paradise Mart on the way to the main road where she was heading to catch the bus, she remembered that Adjoni had an art project.

The note from his teacher read: *Kindly send with your child construction paper and glue for a special art project scheduled for all kindergarten classes.*

It would be pointless, Kayla thought, *to pass this store, go home, borrow Mommy's car, deal with all of its imperfections, and then drive to the other Paradise Mart in Frederiksted.*

She entered the store and headed straight for "Office Supplies". She scoured the aisles carefully. Was she missing something? No. There was no construction paper in sight.

"Where can I find the construction paper?" Kayla interrupted the Paradise Mart associate who was busy watching one movie on all ten display televisions.

"We don't have anymore. You'll have to check our other store in Frederiksted," the associate said. His voice was low and expressionless while his eyes ping-ponged from screen to screen.

Great, so much for trying to avoid the long-winded option.

She'd have to wait for her mom to come home from work so that she could borrow the car. Then the kids would want to come too. Taking her kids into a department store was never, ever fun.

CHAPTER 3

To Richard Patterson, even late January in St. Croix felt like summer in Davenport, Iowa. In fact, it felt like summer all year round, except during the rainy season when it transformed into the dreaded hurricane season (thanks to the trade winds which force tropical storms to put in an appearance). As far as Richard was concerned, hurricanes were really ferocious beasts wrapped up in ominous gray clouds. They showed up faithfully every year, terrorizing everything in their paths.

"Experiencing one will forever change a person's concept of the powers of Nature," he told his family after surviving the last one.

In spite of this, Richard loved St. Croix. He had lived through two of the worst hurricanes, and he was still living on the island.

"It's my haven," he would say to his older brother, Ryder, who expected the novelty to wear off someday soon.

If you asked Richard, the island was an emerald green jewel of gently rolling hills jutting out of the deep blue waters of the Caribbean Sea. He loved the beaches with their turquoise blue waters and soft, glistening, white sand. He was mesmerized by the clear blue sky full of fluffy, white clouds so effortlessly strewn about, thanks to the trade winds which constantly caressed the Caribbean islands.

St. Croix was a long way from Davenport. It was far in the distance, in the population, in the lifestyle, and in the culture. The tiny island, surrounded by the Caribbean Sea, had half the population of Davenport and had been a territory of the United States since 1917. It was previously owned by the English, the Spanish, the French and the Danish, respectively.

St. Croix is the largest of a group of three islands called the U.S. Virgin Islands. Richard was fascinated that the islands were collectively referred to as The American Paradise until he learned the hard way that the U.S. Virgin Islands was no paradise. That realization hit him the day that someone had stolen his 80-piece Wiha™ 32800 Insulated Tool Set from the back of his truck. He couldn't figure out where he had gotten the crazy idea that a $2,000 toolkit would be safe out in the open?

Richard finally had to admit that all of these tiny islands had issues with crime, unemployment, high cost of living and discrimination just like everywhere else on mainland U.S.

All of his tools were now under lock and key.

There was one other difference that Richard had to get used to. The local people dealt with all the undesirable issues on island time. Being late in the islands was expected and accepted. Although the influx of meticulous, time-keeping mainlanders was slowly changing that attitude, the locals still wore the "whatever" look on their faces when they arrived late to an event or an appointment.

Richard moved to St. Croix as an engineer--uptight, driven and over-achieving. Finding work wasn't difficult. There were a few companies on St. Croix and on neighboring St. Thomas that wanted to take him on. He chose *Fenley and Fenley Engineering*. He stuck with them and took over the company two years ago. The Fenleys, both father and son, were engineers for almost thirty years in St. Croix. They had a good reputation as engineers, and they had a good rapport with the locals. Richard learned a lot from them.

Chad Fenley, the son, would take him along to visit his Rastafarian friends in the hills. They would eat Ital, a vegetable stew, and scant to reggae music. Peter Tosh's "Johnny Be Good" would wail in the background while the other activities that were done far away from civilization were carried out among the bushes.

Richard actually tried to make the vegetable stew at home. The recipe seemed simple enough, ingredients: coconut milk, vegetables, and herbal seasonings. *What could be so hard about that?* he thought. Disappointingly, the results were not the same. Richard had to admit that there must be a difference in taste if the stew is cooked in a yabba pot on a wood-burning fire, outside in a grass-swept yard, as opposed to being brewed in a stainless steel pot, on an electric stove in a modern kitchen.

A yabba pot made it on his list of things to purchase. That was another thing he would definitely not find in Davenport, Iowa.

Chad Fenley grew up in St. Croix, and the locals saw him as one of their own. He was white, but somehow he blended in. He married a local woman, and they had three children together. Yvette was Crucian to the core. She wasn't one to hide her roots, and she spoke with a strong Crucian accent which Chad understood perfectly. She had a lean athletic body and was a little shorter than average. Yvette was a beautiful woman with dark chocolate skin and thick, long natural hair. Richard always admired how she carried herself.

Chad and Yvette made sure that their three children were also *down* with the locals, and they took them out of private school for that very purpose.

"These are the people that will look out for them," Chad often said.

He and Yvette contributed heavily to the school, ensuring that their children would get the best education possible. "Other children benefit from our efforts too," Yvette said to Richard when he asked them why they would make such a bold, unconventional move.

The Fenleys had made enough money as engineers in the Virgin Islands to close up shop and comfortably live off their fortune. Brad Fenley, the father, was definitely ready to retire, and Chad said he wanted to spend more time with his family while he still had the energy.

"Take over Rich," encouraged Brad.

"You can do it. I'll be here if you need any advice, but I think you'll be fine," Chad said, hoping Richard would finally say yes. The company had built a good name and reputation. It would be sad to see their legacy disappear. Richard was perfect for the job. He had actually become like family.

When Richard's family came to visit him from Iowa with his ex-girlfriend, Amber, they could not understand his fascination with the island having visited while on a cruise a few years earlier. In fact, that is how Richard learned about St. Croix. When he saw

St. Croix as a port of call, he didn't even know where it was. He had heard of St. Thomas, but he was clueless that the two islands were both part of the U.S. Virgin Islands. He never expected to come back to live. Granted, he was sure he would eventually visit the island again. The slow pace had charmed him. So when his doctor warned him that if he did not slow down he would be dead by forty, he decided to take a break.

"I have to get out of here," Richard told Amber.

"And go where?" Amber asked, imagining some place faster than Davenport. A place with more distractions. A place where she could really be the prima donna she wanted to be.

"I don't know, but I need to get away from this," Richard said.

"And leave all of our friends?" Her voice sounded shrill and passionate.

Friends were always more important to Amber than they were to Richard. She was the typical fortunate girl--beautiful and very hard to please. They were the perfect match (or so everyone said). Amber liked working with kids, but Richard questioned if it was her way of preserving some self-worth. Kids loved her and looked up to her until they were about five or six and then the conversations they had with Amber just didn't make much sense to them anymore.

Richard saw a few ads online and decided to respond. He tried compromising with Amber. "Let's try it out for a year or so, Amb."

"A year! I can never live on an island so far away from North Park Mall."

There were definitely no malls remotely similar on St. Croix, and short of Amber building one herself in the near future, there would be no such structure emerging any time soon.

The text message eventually flashed up on Richard's phone:

"I think we need some time apart to grow."

Richard could imagine the smirk on her face as she wrote those simple words. He had already accepted that the relationship would end. He felt some comfort that he did his best to make sure that the breakup was done quietly. The two would simply disappear out of each other's lives.

In no time, Richard heard that Amber had started seeing Bret Stone, an ex-college football star who, like his girlfriend, was very much into himself. Unfortunately for Amber, Bret had a knee injury that ended his glorious career.

"I should still be receiving royalties, man, and a steady paycheck for all my accomplishments in the four long years that I played," he would quibble time and again.

Bret was certainly Amber's type. Richard could imagine them *growing together*. Richard knew he had only caught Amber's eyes because of what she imagined he had and could be. Although she said it was because he was handsome with a killer physique.

At six-foot-two, Richard had a full muscular frame. His skin was always a little more tanned than his siblings' because he loved to be outdoors. His tanned skin was even darker now that he was living on an island. His hair was sandy blonde which he always kept styled in a textured crew cut. He had soft hazel eyes that Amber said pierced her soul (whatever that meant) and slight bow legs if you looked closely enough. On top of all of that, he was also a top-notch engineer and very driven.

Amber probably reasoned that if Richard kept it up, she could go places. But St. Croix wasn't exactly one of the places she had in mind.

Of course, Richard knew it was all about her.

Richard was now the CEO of *Fenley and Fenley Engineering*. The name remained because it spoke for itself. He had kept Clay as project manager too. Clay Barnes was a young Crucian guy who was on top of his game. He had worked for the Fenleys right out of college, was exceptionally smart, and knew most of the people in construction. In short, Clay knew how to get the job done. Richard would have to be a fool to let him go.

❧

"Give me a timeframe, Clay!" insisted Richard. "I can't go to the clients with another deadline."

"OK. Let me call you back," Clay said, ready to get down on the contractors to demand that they work harder and faster on this project.

"Handle it Clay." Richard hung up.

There were so many stakeholders involved, and everyone's schedule was being pushed back. One of the contractors could not get the plasterwork right, because the client, *Banks and Cohen*, one of the largest law firms on the island, was being very picky about how they wanted the job done.

"Banks and Cohen site visit," Richard painstakingly typed into his phone's calendar. He was dying for this project to be over. It was slowly sapping all of his time and energy. Seeing to it that the last-minute details were taken care of, seemed to drag on for an eternity.

Richard now had to concentrate on the evening ahead of him. He had promised his mom he would call her. It was hard for her to understand that receiving daily phone calls from her thirty-year-old son was not a realistic expectation. He, on the other hand, had to prepare himself for the barrage of questions that would be coming his way. Most of which he would cleverly avoid answering. During the last phone call, Richard found it hard to convince his mother that relaxing on the beach on the small island was a legitimate way to pass the time.

"The beach? That's not recreation," she said. "You need to find something else to do. Don't you have any friends you can hang out with?"

"Yes, a few, Mom."

Of course, Richard wouldn't dare mention his visits to his Rastafarian friends in the hills. His mother would certainly be horrified and keel over, and he wanted to keep her around for as long as possible. He promised to call her at seven o'clock sharp in the evening, and there was no way Richard was going to miss that appointment. He had already mustered up all the courage he needed to make the call today. There would be no postponing.

Before the important mother/son phone call could occur, though, Richard had to make a stop at the Big Paradise Mart on the western side of the island. Although the Paradise Mart in Sunny Isle was closer, both Paradise Marts didn't carry all of the same products. Of course, Richard knew that it was the company's business strategy. That was how they got customers to visit both stores.

At first, Richard felt that everything on the island was close by. "St. Croix is only eighty-four square miles," he would say to people who complained about distance. That being said, Richard had slowly started adopting the locals' relative concept of distance. In Davenport, a forty-five-minute drive was close by. On St. Croix, however, a forty-five-minute drive is considered so far that most people would think twice about making the trip.

Richard's office was located in Christiansted on the eastern side of the island and the Paradise Mart he wanted to go to was in Frederiksted on the western side of the island. He really didn't have a choice. Besides, for Richard, driving his *Ford F-150 Raptor*™ from one end of the island to the other wouldn't exactly be a snooze fest. He adored the liquid blue exterior, EcoBoost engine under the hood, 3.5-liter V-6 with twin turbochargers and direct fuel injection, tons of torque, and at least 450 ponies. It would be a sweet ride. All Richard had to do was decide on whether he would take the much-traveled Centerline Road which would be crawling with traffic or the Melvin H. Evans Highway, which would be a straight shot. Richard settled on giving his *Raptor*™ a chance to stretch its legs on the open four-lane highway. Then a quick in and out of Paradise Mart would leave just enough time to get home, take a shower, cook some pasta, and still make the dreaded phone call to his dear mother.

CHAPTER 4

Just as Kayla suspected, her kids would not be left at home while she headed to Paradise Mart.

"Adjoni, if you are coming with me, then, where are your shoes?" Kayla breathed and closed her eyes shut for a quick second.

It was impossible to leave the house without the drama of changing a shirt or finding a shoe or parting with a toy that would definitely not be tagging along only to get lost somewhere.

Most toys that left the house never made the return trip home.

Finally, they made it out the door and down the stairwell.

"Daddy!" Samaria and Adjoni screamed as they saw their father sitting on the smoke-filled steps in front of them.

Kayla didn't share their excitement, but that was their father. The man she had chosen. She rubbed her temples and decided to suck it up.

"Where you guys going all dressed up?" their absentee father asked with squinted red, cloudy eyes. He had been the last one to haul on the marijuana joint that was being passed around from one guy to the next.

"Paradise Mart," they cried in unison.

"Don't forget your Daddy when you get there. Bring me back something nice," he said with a wide grin.

Years ago, Kayla noticed that Omari's lips were getting darker since he had become a regular smoker. "This is how man get wisdom, right here," he would say to her sometimes. Kayla would lift her chin and say, "All right, then." *Imagine, this dude is totally convinced that his new habit of staying high for the whole day was turning him into some kind of sage,* she would think.

Omari's silly request brought a response on the tip of Kayla's tongue, and she wasn't convinced that she could control herself and hold it in.

Glimpsing the sneer on Omari's cloudy face erased any likelihood of controlling her mouth. "Give them some money to help them remember you." Her words gushed out like water from a busted pipe.

"Daddy loves you," Omari said, reassuring his kids and ignoring their mother's wisecrack.

"We love you too, Daddy," they said.

After a few quick hugs and kisses, they waved goodbye and were on their way to the parking lot where Margo's 1988 *Honda Accord*™ awaited them. The *Accord*™ was fully-loaded, power everything. Kayla still clearly remembered the day her mother brought the car home. Margo had been taking driving lessons for a year and had finally gotten her license after three tries at the DMV.

It was a happy day.

No more long walks to catch the bus and long walks back with grocery bags. Every Saturday, religiously, Margo trooped with Kayla and Mally to the grocery store. Each would be assigned at least two bags. It was almost twelve years ago, but forgetting those days was hard. The Honda™ was a used car, but a car nonetheless.

Sad to say, now all of its power was fading like an old, washed-up superhero. For long distances the windows could be put down low enough so no one suffocated; but if it was a short ride, the semi-working air conditioner needed to be on full blast. Paradise Mart was far enough to put the windows down, and Kayla was prepared to spend the extra 10 minutes needed in the parking lot to coax the windows back up.

The parking lot of the Paradise Mart store was full, as usual. Amazingly, with the exception of the Paradise Mart stores in the U.S. Virgin Islands, the big-box department stores were closing its doors all over the U.S. However, here in St. Croix this was all that the locals had, and they were intent on keeping the doors open.

Richard pulled into the Paradise Mart lot and saw a spot close to the entrance. Lamentably, he was not the only driver eyeing the space. A black Honda *Accord*™ traveling in the opposite direction beat him to it and got in nice and straight.

As their mother struggled to get the windows up, Samaria and Adjoni could feel the speech coming. They knew the drill.

It was a ritual.

"I only have money for your art project--," Kayla started almost out of breath, then she continued, "--so don't ask for anything else. It's OK if you want to go see all the toys, but remember that we are only here to buy the paper and glue for Adjoni's art project. Understood?"

"Yes, Mommy," they both said.

With heads down, the two kids eyed each other and smirked.

Everyone in the car knew that the well-prepared speech was useless. This was "Big Paradise Mart" with all the bells and whistles, more products than the Paradise Mart located in Sunny Isles, more space for clothing, furniture, accessories, and even a pharmacy. There would most certainly be a whole lot of begging once they got inside.

Samaria and Adjoni loved Paradise Mart. They would say, "But Mommy it's like a playground with bright white floors instead of green grass. No trees, just tall shelves packed with lots of fun stuff to buy."

The toy section was right next to Office Supplies. That was good and bad for Kayla. Good, because she would not have to trek across the whole store so that her kids could browse all of the toys that they had already seen. Bad, because it could not be avoided.

"We need to get your construction paper and glue first, Adjoni," Kayla reminded her son. "Remember that this is your art project, not mine."

With construction paper and glue in hand, Kayla was ready to check out and leave. Naturally, she would have to give her kids some time to browse the toy section for the umpteenth time. Her day was long and tiring and not yet over. She had actually gotten the job, and she was thrilled. Imagine, Kayla Jackson was going to work in the morning. Yet, she had to get the kids ready for bed and ready for school the next day. She also had to get herself ready and think about what she was going to wear to work. Kayla scanned her closet in her mind as her children oohed and awed over every single toy in each aisle.

Richard entered Paradise Mart with a plan--head straight to the back, grab what he needed and split. He needed a large plastic bin-

-that was it. Men don't browse, he always reminded Amber. Most men hate shopping, and he was proud to be part of that club.

Richard's renovation was unpredictable. This was the fifth, and hopefully, the final bin he would need to buy. He wanted all of them in black, just in case uniformity was important at some point. If this Paradise Mart didn't have it, he might have to try the hardware store. But he was hoping it would be here. Another stop was just out of the question, and he needed the bin tonight.

Once Richard got to the back of the store, he saw a Paradise Mart associate realigning some dark green bins. "Any black ones?" Richard asked, hoping the answer would be yes.

The associate turned around surprised at the question. "Yes, in the back," he said frustrated and turned his back to Richard once again.

"Can I get one?" Richard asked, noticing that there was no desire nor was there any offer to retrieve the black bin he wanted.

"I'll have to go all the way in the back for it. You sure you don't want to take one of the green ones?" the associate asked.

"Yes, I'm sure I want a black one," Richard said. Black was the color he wanted. He was the guy who made sure the job was done--the right way. Richard wasn't a half-stepper. Maybe that's why engineering appealed to him. He had a penchant for finding solutions to technical problems; and he didn't give up easily--another reason why he always butted heads with his parents and siblings.

Upset with the pressure that Richard was putting on him, the associate shook his head and went through the double doors leading to the warehouse.

The associate, Ron, was a short, older white guy with a familiar and somewhat puckish face. He was obviously retired from some other job. Now working at Paradise Mart, but not necessarily look-ing for more work.

Ron struggled through the double doors pulling two large black bins behind him.

"Just in case this picky guy decides to take two, I'm gonna save myself the time and trouble of returning to the hot, dark warehouse to fight with bins that are almost as tall as me," he said to himself.

The annoying customer did decide to take the two bins, and Ron was proud of himself for thinking ahead. He made no offer to help take a bin to the front, and he hoped the customer was not expect-ing one either. Ron defiantly headed back to the warehouse.

"He's a tall guy; he'll figure it out," Ron snarled as the doors closed behind him.

Richard was left abandoned on the sales floor, encumbered by the two huge black bins. In spite of this, he skillfully navigated the bins through the aisles, eventually arriving at the counter of a not-so-busy cashier. There was one customer at the counter with two restless kids, obviously unhappy that this was their last lap in the store.

"That will be $11.99," he heard the Paradise Mart cashier tell the lady.

"But it should be on sale," the lady challenged.

It was clear to Richard that there was a problem with a price, and the customer was adamant. She was disputing it. *What could possibly be the problem with construction paper and glue?* Richard thought.

"Well, that's not what it says in the system." The cashier ex-haled. She placed her mouth right up to the microphone connected to her cash register. "Price check please!" she screamed.

Richard tapped his fingers on one of the bin covers and contemplated changing cashiers, but with one bin in front and one behind and a long line quickly forming behind him he was stuck.

"This really can't be happening." Richard exhaled into his closed fist.

As everyone waited for an associate to go to the back of the store to verify the price in the Office Supplies section, there were some disappointing sighs. Richard tried to avoid looking at the woman who was making his In-and-Out-of-Paradise-Mart Plan a little more difficult. He could see that she was shaking her head in frustration. He was tempted to give her the difference. *How much could it be? A dollar--or two?* he thought.

Then, she eyeballed everyone with her hands folded in front of her with a "Do-you-have-a-problem-with-me-demanding-the-sale-price?" look on her face.

All eyes turned away.

Each one in the line knew that at some point they had all done the same thing and would do it again if they had to. Richard tried not to make eye contact, but he felt her eyes waiting for his support. He decided that he should at least look up to give her a nod.

"It's OK. I would do the same thing too," Richard mumbled and fake-smiled.

Then came an exaggerated rolling of the eyes and pursing of her full lips. Richard saw that the lady seemed satisfied.

Kayla exhaled. *All these people would have done the same thing, including this man in the cap behind me,* she thought.

At this point, she seemed to be the only one getting any satisfaction from this production--apart from her children who also didn't seem to mind spending a few more minutes in the store. Kayla was praying that the sale sign she saw was in fact tagged for the construction paper she had on the counter. Ten dollars was all she had--nothing else. It would be an embarrassment to have to leave without the construction paper because she didn't have two extra dollars. Kayla tried not to let the uneasiness show on her face.

"How much time could it possibly take to get to the Office Supply section to check a price?" Richard grumbled, his patience slowly running out.

He looked up again when he felt it was safe. At first, all he saw was the back of her head. Her hair was pulled back in a ponytail that was full of coiling twists at the ends. Her face was a blur when she looked at him during their short validation session. But now he was beginning to see her profile. She looked over at him again with wide anxious eyes; this time biting her lips, almost apologizing for the wait.

Richard imagined Clay's words, "She gotta have the 3 B's, brah--Beauty, Brains, and Body. You know wha' I'm saying?" Then he could hear Clay go on his usual tangent about women. Richard could see that this one right here was beautiful. She was about five foot six or seven, had smooth mocha skin, and a perfect fine-boned face with dark almond-shaped eyes. There was no doubt about her looks. She was good-looking.

Brains?

Well, he couldn't be sure. She was demanding the sale price, if that meant anything.

Body?

It would be creepy if I scan her this close, he thought. *If she caught me eyeing her, she would think I was some kind of pervert.* Richard resorted to waiting until she walked away.

But two children? That could only mean one thing--some guy was lurking around somewhere. A husband? He didn't see a ring. *A baby daddy* or two? *That would just be too much drama for my humdrum existence,* Richard contemplated. *I'm definitely not going there. I didn't come to St. Croix to chill out, only to get caught up in that mess. That would do me in for sure.*

The associate finally came back with the sale price. Problem solved. Relieved, the mother paid for her goods. She grabbed her bag and her kids and marched out of the store leaving a strong berry scent lingering in the air.

Richard peeked at the young lady as she walked away.

Yep, she definitely has the last 'B'.

CHAPTER 5

Kayla's first day at work was unbelievable. She actually had a real job. A working woman, walking into the location where she would now be spending most of her days. Mrs. Merchant was the first person to greet her. It seemed as if her new boss had dreamed of this second encounter.

Her sunny greeting was almost blinding. "Good Morning, Ms. Jackson. I hope you slept well and came prepared to work," Mrs. Merchant said.

"Good morning, Mrs. Merchant. Yes, I came prepared to work," Kayla said, managing to crack a smile. Kayla couldn't say that she had slept well. Sleeping with two kids in a full-sized bed had a funny way of ruining REM sleep. Her kids had their own room with their own beds, but somehow they both always made it into her room in the middle of the night. "Mommy, move over," she would hear them whisper in her ears. From that moment on, her sleep would be forever interrupted.

"So, let's start here," Mrs. Merchant began. "I'll introduce you to the staff. This is Shameka. She makes sure that the pantry is stocked. We can't afford to run out of food. We have a lot of mouths to feed."

"Nice to meet you," Kayla said politely. Kayla remembered Shameka's remark when she came in the day before to apply for the job, and she was hoping there would be no drama. But with a name like Shameka that might be wishful thinking.

"And this is Pedro," Mrs. Merchant went on. "Pedro preps and cooks some of the dishes. He does a mean macaroni pie too. Shameka and Pedro serve food to our customers as well. We cook for our patients, but anyone can buy food from our cafeteria. Our head chefs, Mr. Sutton and Mrs. Nunez are in the kitchen. Let me take you inside to them."

"Nice to meet you." Kayla nodded in acknowledgment that one, she understood the job descriptions and two, she recognized that there was a Shameka/Pedro tag team to boot.

Noted.

The industrial kitchen was clean, orderly, and fairly large. Kayla was actually surprised and impressed. Apparently, Mrs. Merchant ran a tight ship. The two cooks were busy getting ready for lunch and didn't have much time to chit chat. The nutritionist, Belle, had just finished going over a few points with them about some patients with special diets.

"Let's talk about what you will be doing around here," pointed out Mrs. Merchant. "Pedro needs help prepping and cooking. Shameka has enough on her plate trying to keep up with stocking the kitchen. Pedro will train you, so don't worry. Uniforms are over there in the closet. You can check to see what size fits. You look like a medium. You can wear a full uniform or you can wear black pants with the kitchen staff shirt."

Mrs. Merchant went on and on about punctuality, teamwork, and cleanliness. Kayla got the message, but of course, she wouldn't dare to interrupt her new boss. Her mind wandered on the uniform. She would have loved to choose the full uniform, but the pants were white. Cleaning them would be a nightmare. She opted to wear black pants with a staff shirt. She had at least six pairs of black pants. That would be her uniform.

Mrs. Merchant took Kayla to the lab for blood work. Unbeknownst to Kayla, a necessary evil before being issued a Food Handlers Certificate which was required in order to work around food for public consumption. Following this painful and totally unexpected episode, Mrs. Merchant proceeded to give a quick tour of the entire hospital.

"You need to know your territory," Mrs. Merchant said looking Kayla straight in the eye. She took Kayla outside to show her the site for the new Diabetes Center. "We are in dire need of a center that can treat diabetic patients. This Center will have training rooms designed for special seminars to teach diabetics how to manage the disease."

"I see," said Kayla, hoping to show her interest in the subject.

After walking around for about an hour while Mrs. Merchant gave her opinion about the administration and the staff, they went through another set of double doors that opened to a corridor with rows of doors on both sides. Mrs. Merchant gently tapped on the door marked "HR 1". She opened the door halfway but kept most of her body outside. "Hi, Brenda. I have new staff for you."

"Okay, Merchie. I'll take care of her," a voice said.

"Thanks." Mrs. Merchant opened the door wider to allow Kayla to enter the office. "Brenda will take care of you. There's a lot of paperwork and information we need from you."

"Okay," said Kayla.

"Once you're done, please come to my office." Mrs. Merchant smiled and closed the door behind her.

The HR 1 office was tiny. There was only enough room for one small desk and two visitor chairs that were pushed right up against a wall that didn't go all the way up to the ceiling. Brenda was tall and seemed to be uncomfortable in her cramped quarters. All the papers she needed were in a file organizer attached to the wall next to the desk.

Brenda handed Kayla a five-page booklet. "Please fill out the information as accurately and as clearly as possible. The hospital will need bank account numbers for direct deposit, home addresses, telephone numbers, names in case of emergency, medical history, and other information for insurance purposes."

Mrs. Merchant's spacious office was on the other side of the hospital. Fortunately, it was part of the tour, so Kayla figured out how to find her way back there. She knocked gently and entered as the sign on the door instructed. There were large glass windows that revealed a view of the bushy lot behind the hospital. Enough visitor chairs were strewn about just in case there was a need for a small staff meeting, but most were occupied with papers.

"Please have a seat," Mrs. Merchant said as Kayla entered.

Kayla looked around and sat down in the one free visitor chair.

"Now, let me tell you about the LPN course," Mrs. Merchant said staring at Kayla. "It's a twelve-month, state-approved training program. The majority of learning is completed in a classroom setting."

It seemed to Kayla that the LPN topic was on Mrs. Merchant's mind ever since Kayla showed up for work this morning. "Where will the classes be held?" Kayla asked.

"The classes are held here in our meeting rooms," Mrs. Merchant said, sensing Kayla's need for reassurance.

"At night?" Kayla asked. She was skeptical, but she feigned optimism.

"Some of the classes are held during working hours and some are held at night depending on the availability of the professors. Upon completion of your LPN program, you will receive an associate degree or certificate, usually required by the government for testing," Mrs. Merchant said.

"It sounds interesting," Kayla said, trying to digest everything.

Mrs. Merchant continued, "Once you've completed the LPN program, you must pass the National Council of State Boards of Nursing (NCSBN) exam ..."

Then Kayla heard something about an "NCLEX-PN exam." Then, there was a part about having forty-five days to retake the exam. At length, Kayla heard, "...free to pursue employment as an LPN here at the hospital. There will be positions open for any staff who successfully complete the program."

To make a long story short, Kayla didn't understand much of what Mrs. Merchant had said. What she did catch, however, were the words "Associates Degree" and "Certificate". That section on every job application had stumped her for years. "College/University" flashed into her mind.

"When does the program start?" Kayla was curious.

"The first class started a week ago, but you can catch up. I know the organizers. I'm sure they can still squeeze you in," Mrs. Merchant said, grinning and offering to pull some strings.

"I'll need to know when classes are held at night. I have two children," Kayla said, deciding to reveal that tidbit of information. It seemed like the right time to discuss her children. If Kayla started taking this course, her mother would have to be willing to babysit Samaria and Adjoni. Margo also had exercise classes on some weeknights, and her mother was the only person Kayla trusted with her children. If Margo wasn't willing, then this LPN course would be out of the question.

"Let me get the details for you, and I'll let you know before the day is over," Mrs. Merchant promised.

At eleven forty-five they walked back to the kitchen where the lunchtime buzz was well on its way. There was already a long line in the cue. Pedro looked up at Kayla as she entered the cafeteria with Mrs. Merchant.

"Go wash your hands," he commanded. "We have work to do."

Mrs. Merchant smiled and said, "I'll leave you in Pedro's capable hands."

"Put these gloves on and cover your head with this hair net. There's an apron over there that you can use," he continued.

The title of the old TV show "Charles in Charge" ran through Kayla's mind. Pedro seemed to be relishing his role as a drill sergeant, and Kayla was the new recruit.

"We need help on the serving line. Use the utensil in front of each dish. One serving per dish. Any questions?" Pedro snarled.

"Yes, a lot," Kayla wanted to say, but "Got it!" came out humbly.

Kayla felt awkward serving food in the cafeteria. There were more people coming into the cafeteria than she had anticipated. All she could do was to point at the board when people asked her about what was on the menu. She had no intention of asking Pedro any questions unless it was absolutely necessary.

CHAPTER 6

It was twelve-forty when Richard's phone beeped. "Hey Rich!" The text message flashed up on his screen.

What now? Richard thought.

It was Clay.

"You meeting with the Mac at the hospital or what?" Clay paused for effect.

"Yes, I'm on my way," Richard replied, knowing that he had completely forgotten about his meeting with Mr. McAllister, the hospital administrator. They were supposed to discuss the new Diabetes Center. He had arranged the meeting himself, but he was so caught up with negotiating a new deadline for the Banks and Cohen project that this meeting had completely slipped his mind.

The meeting was scheduled for one o'clock. "I'll be there in ten minutes," Richard puffed and ran his fingers through his hair.

Clay knew Richard had forgotten. That's why he had sent the text message twenty minutes before. They always tried to get to meetings ten minutes early, to chat a little and compose themselves.

When Richard arrived, Clay was in the parking lot waiting faithfully, leaning against his Barcelona Red V-6 4 x 4 Toyota Tacoma™ pickup which he affectionately called "Big T".

"What's up, man?" Clay asked Richard as they bumped fists.

"Thanks for the text, bro," Richard said, grateful for the reminder.

"You forgot, right?" Clay said chuckling and shaking his head. "That's why I'm here, man."

"Did you see the space yet?" Richard asked, looking over at the proposed site.

"I haven't been inside. I was waiting for you to show up."

"All right. Let's go." Richard rubbed his hands as if trying to warm them. This was not a meeting he wanted to be late for. The two proceeded toward the hospital entrance to meet with the hospital administrator.

John McAllister, was a tall, stately retired doctor. He was a Crucian by birth, but had lived for some time in Michigan. His accent was indistinguishable at times, so it was literally hard to place him on the U.S. map. The man had a penchant for punctuality. Richard knew that and still had the nerve to forget all about this meeting.

As Richard and Clay got closer to the entrance, they saw the tall figure standing erect on the other side of the automatic glass sliding doors. The face was staid and aristocratic. The Mac was waiting for them. It was now one o'clock on the dot.

"Gentlemen," Mr. McAllister greeted his two visitors with an air of formality.

"How are you, Mr. McAllister?" Richard asked politely, trying to avoid any discussion about punctuality.

Clay stood behind Richard and let his boss take the lead on this one. He wasn't as diplomatic as Richard was.

"I was beginning to wonder if you were still coming," Mr. McAllister said, redirecting the conversation to the issue at hand--punctuality.

It sounded to Richard like the administrator was about to lecture them, but Richard decided not to comment. He preferred not to go down that road. Part of diplomacy was knowing which battles deserved his energy. This was not one of them.

"Did you guys already have lunch?" Mr. McAllister asked, wanting to show off the cafeteria's lunch menu. He was certain that today was the perfect day to do it.

Lunch was the furthest thing from Richard's mind. His whole morning had been spent on the phone with different people trying to resolve issues. Clay had a *Cubano* sandwich from *Victor Menchos*, but he could always make room for more.

"Let's see if we can find a table in the caf. We can eat and discuss a few things before heading to the site."

Mr. McAllister led the way. First, to the left. Then, through some gray double doors. The place was packed, but there was always one metal table with four chairs in the back left corner reserved for Mr. McAllister and his guests just in case he decided to invite someone for lunch. He never needed to stand in line, of course. He was the hospital administrator. The menu was always brought to him.

Pedro noticed the big boss walk into the cafeteria with two guests. "Carry this menu to that table over there," he barked at Kayla.

"Huh?...OK," Kayla said and scrambled over to the three diners, holding the menu as if it were a precious newborn baby. As she got closer to the table, she wasn't sure who in the group should receive the laminated list of lunch options. There was a tall, stately man in a suit and two other men; one white and one black, both casually dressed. She deduced that the suit should receive the package.

"Good afternoon," Kayla said, greeting everyone at the table. "He--Here you go, sir." She stuttered and presented the menu to the diner in the suit. One look at his strict face and Kayla was sure she had made the right choice.

Out of nowhere, Mrs. Merchant appeared behind Kayla as if she was trying to intercept the "Who are you?" look on the hospital administrator's enquiring face. "Mr. McAllister, this is Kayla Jackson our new staff," she said. "This is her first day with us. She will also be signing up for the LPN Certificate Program which you conceptualized."

"Wonderful!" Mr. McAllister's face was beaming. Everyone could tell that this was not a normal occurrence. His face muscles were trembling in shock at his expression of delight. "Well, I hope you enjoy it here," Mr. McAllister continued. "We strive for excellence, you know."

Although Mr. McAllister was quite amusing, Clay was more interested in the new recruit. Where was she from? He was Crucian and knew lots of people. The island wasn't that big. Why had he never seen her before? Richard, on the other hand, instantly recognized the face and the faint fruity aroma of berries. Even with the hairnet and apron, he couldn't mistake her. Last night she was wearing dark blue jeans and a red t-shirt that read "Black Beauty". Today, he wasn't sure what was behind the apron, but she was still captivating. Kayla took their orders and Shameka did the honors of delivering their choices.

"We need to refill the drink station with straws and napkins," Pedro told Kayla. His words were, in fact, a command for her to refill the drink station.

"Where do I get the straws and napkins from?" Kayla asked looking around her new workspace, attempting to answer her own question.

"Look under the cabinet," Pedro growled as if Kayla should have known this stuff in view of her hour-long employment in the cafeteria.

As Kayla searched for the straws and napkins to refill the drink station, Richard made his way over. Instantly, the strong fresh scent of juicy berries took him back to Paradise Mart. It really was the only pleasant taste from the entire ordeal. Richard didn't plan to say anything to the young lady who had made his visit to Paradise Mart a little too exciting for his liking. He really just needed some more napkins, in fact, lots of napkins, since Mr. McAllister had convinced him to get the ribs and macaroni pie. "The juiciest ribs you'll ever taste," he had said to Richard.

"Let me get some more napkins for you," Kayla offered the patron that showed up at the drink station. Out of nowhere, she got a whiff of summertime in a woodland full of wildflowers and orange leaves. The scent was surprisingly familiar.

"So how did the art project turn out?" Richard teased as he took the handful of napkins that were offered to him.

"What?" Kayla asked, frowning and puzzled at the question from this stranger.

"The art project. You bought construction paper and glue last night, right?" Richard said, realizing she had no clue who he was.

"Excuse me?" Kayla peered at the man standing in front of her.

"I was one of the customers you held hostage until you got your sale price." Richard raised his palms at her to show that he came in peace and meant no harm.

"Really?" Kayla chuckled. "Sorry, I wanted my discount." Her voice lowered. "Actually, I needed a discount. I had just enough money," she admitted, "and I-I couldn't disappoint my son."

"Well, I was the person right behind you," Richard said, reminding her.

"You mean in the cap, sandwiched between the two black garbage bins?" She hadn't remembered the face, but the cologne was hard to forget.

"Yes, that was me." Richard bowed his head slightly.

"OK. Well, I didn't mean to hold you hostage," Kayla said, biting her lip.

Richard remembered that same apologetic look in her eyes the night before in the store. Today, her beautifully low and soft voice drew him in. "It's okay. Thanks for the napkins," he said and smiled at her.

"No problem." She smiled back.

Richard walked back to his seat amused. He could feel the muscles in his face forming a faint smile. As he sat down, he tried to avoid the questions in Clay's probing eyes.

"So what, you know her?" Clay asked through his teeth.

"Met her in Paradise Mart last night," whispered Richard.

"And..." Clay pried for more.

"And nothing. She has two kids," Richard said, biting off a piece of meat from his rib bone.

"And ...?" Clay stared at Richard.

Richard used a napkin to mop up saucy juice from his chin. "Remember you said 'no baby momma drama?'" he said without looking up.

"I know what I said, but the 3 B's man!"

"Yes, I know--Beauty, Brains and Body," Richard said as he eyed the heavy-set Hispanic guy make his way over to the drink station.

Clay looked at his boss, shook his head and returned to eating his macaroni pie. As far as he was concerned, this conversation wasn't over.

"Talking too much over here," Pedro said to Kayla. "You are here to work, not chat."

"I was only--," Kayla started to explain. "Got it," she decided to say. This was a battle she would not win. On top of that, this was her first day of work.

Kayla finished her assigned task of refilling the drink station under Pedro's strict supervision from across the room. The cafeteria was emptying slowly which allowed her to get some more tables cleaned.

The administrator left with his two guests without Kayla noticing. She cleaned their table and went back into the kitchen to finish washing the dishes. Once that was done, Pedro instructed her that the floors also needed to be mopped.

CHAPTER 7

Kayla's first day of work was the usual *first day*-- a lot to learn and many different personalities to work with. Pedro seemed intent on breaking her, but he was no match for Omari. If Omari failed, Pedro wouldn't stand a chance. Shameka seemed to be warming up to her a little, but Kayla wasn't sure where that was coming from so she decided to keep a safe distance. The cooks were always busy. Belle, the nutritionist, was always in her office. But Mrs. Merchant--she was special. Kayla was still trying to figure her out. Why was Mrs. Merchant so interested in seeing her succeed? Her boss knew nothing about her. In fact, they had just met.

The long bus ride home was as expected--a tight fit of too many hot, tired, sweaty people all with the same destination in mind.

Home. Once the bus let her off at the gas station on the corner, Kayla still had the long haul down the road to her dingy apartment building. Fortunately for her, Ms. Bishop would have already gone home for the day. Unfortunately, she couldn't expect the same from Omari. He would probably still be sitting outside. Those guys only left the steps to relieve themselves, and sometimes even that duty was taken care of in the vicinity. The possibility of another encounter with Omari made Kayla frown.

On her walk home, Kayla's thoughts ran to the conversation she had had with the garbage bin guy who stood behind her at the Paradise Mart check-out counter the night before. Based on what he said, she was convinced that she had made a real spectacle of herself. She imagined that she was so obvious that he could not forget her. But never mind, it was all for her son, and she would do it again.

Kayla wondered how she could have missed the refined handsome face that she saw again in the cafeteria. In reality, she had not focused on any of the faces of the people who were in the line that night. Nonetheless, he had been standing right behind her. She did remember looking at him, but he had avoided making eye contact. Now, she thought about how nice looking he was, definitely in his late twenties or early thirties. He was tall, not basketball player tall, but tall nonetheless. He was well-built too, but besides all this, he was really funny. She was amused when he raised his palms at her to show that he came in peace. His voice was deep and pleasant.

Margo was folding clothes on the couch when Kayla entered the apartment.

"So, how was your first day?" Margo asked, praying that the response would be positive. She really wanted her daughter to accomplish something in her life. There was no doubt in her mind that Kayla had a lot of potential, and she didn't feel that way just because she was her mother. Kayla always got good grades. She loved to read and loved to write. She won three awards for essays in elementary school and one in high school. It wasn't until after she started hanging out with Omari that everything went downhill.

There was no need for Margo to remind Kayla about her bad decisions in the past. Kayla was living with the consequences every day.

"It was good. A lot to learn," Kayla said, trying to sound positive knowing it would please her mother. In reality, she had no problem with the job. In fact, the thought of finally being able to support her kids without begging for help was thrilling.

Relieved at Kayla's positive response Margo said, "Most jobs are challenging in the beginning."

"Mrs. Merchant spoke with me about an LPN course that the hospital is offering the staff. She wants me to consider applying for it, but I'll see," Kayla said and briefed her mother on more of the day's activities.

"So what have you decided?" Margo was dying to know what was going through her daughter's mind about the course.

"Well, I wanted to discuss it with you," Kayla told her mother. "There is one night class every Tuesday. I know you have your exercise class on Wednesdays, but will you be willing to babysit Adjoni and Samaria for me on Tuesdays?" Kayla continued as if in deep thought. "Then I might need a ride home on Tuesdays. I don't want to walk to the Centerline at ten o'clock at night." Turning over all of the logistics in her mind, she ended by saying, "I really don't want to put more on your plate. You do so much for me already, Mommy."

Margo did a good job keeping back her tears. She was actually thrilled that Kayla would have an opportunity to become a nurse. That had always been her daughter's dream. Growing up, Kayla would often pretend to be a nurse with all of her dolls; and even animals if her mother let her.

Yet, Margo sensed apprehension. Kayla wasn't the confident, self-assured person she had been as a child. It was almost as if she had given up on her dreams. Margo knew the feeling. It had happened to her too. She had always dreamed of becoming a teacher, but there were many disappointments. "Kayla, I will be willing to babysit for you on Tuesdays. The kids would love the ride."

"It will be a lot of studying." Kayla shook her head in defeat.

"Are you afraid? Afraid to fail?" Margo asked meeting Kayla's eyes.

"Maybe," Kayla said, looking down at her feet.

Margo held her daughter's hand tightly. She herself had never gotten any support. Her life was one wretched mistake after the other. Her kids could do better. She would help them to achieve their goals. "Kayla, do you remember the quote you used to have pasted on your bedroom wall? The one that said something about not failing if your determination to succeed is strong."

"I forgot all about that quote," Kayla said shocked that her mother had remembered it. The piece of paper with the quote in her twelve-year-old handwriting had long since fallen off of her bedroom wall, in fact, years ago.

Kayla did remember the way the quote made her feel every time she walked into her bedroom. When had she stopped feeling that way? The desire to dream and succeed had faded a long, long time ago. Kayla would have to sleep on it. She really didn't want to start anything that she wouldn't be able to finish.

"I'll think about it," Kayla said.

Margo didn't want to pressure her daughter. She always tried to encourage Kayla to make her own decisions and understand lessons about consequences, but this time was different. "You will be taking the course, Kayla," Margo declared to her daughter. "Sign up for it tomorrow."

"I'll have to buy books too, Mommy. Those books cost so much money." Kayla was protesting, but she didn't know why. She was sure that the argument would end in her mother's favor.

"Did you hear what I said? You will be taking the LPN course. We will find a way to pay for the books. You have a job now. We will make sure your course books are included in our budget."

Kayla could feel a Margo Plan coming on. She would not be surprised if her mother called Mrs. Merchant to ask about financial aid. Usually schools offer aid to students who are underprivileged. This was a hospital program, but Margo would try anything. Whether Kayla got financial aid or not, she knew that her mother would make sure that she took this course. Kayla believed that Margo was even prepared to call her father, Kenrick. He had agreed to help Mally with the books for his first year of college, but what he put her mother through to get that money was nothing less than humiliating. Margo basically had to grovel. Imagine, Kenrick had not given them a dime since he left them high and dry when Mally was five years old. Now, he acted like a Superhero Dad for helping with a few books.

Kenrick wouldn't get the satisfaction of helping me, Kayla thought. *Let him keep his stinking money.* "We'll work something out," Kayla said in a soft, audible voice.

Thankfully, the Benhams had given Mally a plane ticket as a graduation gift, and he qualified for financial aid. He was accepted into MIT and was now studying architecture, just as he had dreamed all his life. Margo was determined to keep Malik off of those awful steps outside the building no matter what it took.

"Look at your brother. He is doing something with his life. I want the same for you, Kayla."

"I know, Mommy," Kayla said, knowing full well that her older brother was no saint. Their mother would never be told that he had already pulled on a weed joint several times behind the building-- almost choking to death the first time he tried. Nor would she ever find out about the time when he wolfed down two cookies baked with marijuana and was passed out for the rest of the afternoon. Margo just assumed that he was coming down with the flu. Mally and Kayla were all she had, and they knew that she was determined that her children make something of themselves even if she didn't have much to offer besides hope, support, and encouragement.

Kayla knew her mother was serious. She saw the same look on Margo's face when she had announced that she was dropping out of high school because she had become pregnant. Kayla could not forget those days.

"You gon' get your high school diploma. You not dropping out of high school. You hear me?" Margo had told her.

Kayla had finished high school and graduated with honors when she was five months pregnant with Samaria. She was still grateful to her mother for pushing her and never giving up on her.

Kayla looked at her mother and smiled. "So it's settled. I'll be taking the LPN course. I'll let Mrs. Merchant know tomorrow."

CHAPTER 8

Two days after meeting with Mr. McAllister, Clay barged into Richard's office. "So what's up with you and your friend from Paradise Mart?" Clay was insisting on more concrete answers now that he and Richard were back in the office and could talk freely.

"It was just small talk." Richard held back, actually enjoying every moment that he kept Clay in suspense.

"Give me a break, Richard. Small talk don't involve that much smiling." Clay frowned knowing his boss was stringing him along.

"Stop tripping, Clay. It was nothing. Calm down. What's the big deal anyway? I already told you she has two kids."

"What makes you think they couldn't have been her niece and nephew?"

"Aww...because they called her 'Mommy'."

"So, there's no chance, not the tiniest possibility?" Clay said as he illustrated a gap of about an inch between his thumb and index finger.

Richard lifted his head and looked Clay in the eyes. "No chance."

"OK. Whatever you say."

Richard was adamant. He wasn't going there. There was no way he would be starting a relationship with someone who had two kids. Absolutely not! Her being Crucian wasn't the problem. He actually felt attracted to the women in St. Croix. He thought they were good- looking and had a Caribbean swagger that made them exceptionally appealing. The one he met in Paradise Mart had it, but she also had two kids--two! That was a game-changer. Richard didn't mind having kids someday, but he did not want someone else's problem.

"Let's go over what we got for the Diabetes Center," Richard said, changing the subject. He could tell that Clay wouldn't mind talking about this stuff all day, but they had work to do. Not only that, it really didn't make sense to waste time on a non-issue. "Oh, before I forget to tell you, *Banks and Cohen* is having an office party this Friday, and they invited us. You game?"

"Food and drinks? Yeh man, I'm game. Where?"

"The Galley."

"Food always on point. I'll be there."

The Galley was a cool spot to hang out. It was a nice place to take family and friends who were visiting. The seafood was always delicious. In fact, everything on the menu was good. The restaurant was owned by a local family from the area in Gallows Bay. It had been in the family for years, with each generation growing up, learning the business, and taking their place to keep making it happen. The restaurant was always packed with locals and visitors alike.

"On your way out, please ask Marisol to call and confirm. They needed that confirmation yesterday. Jason Banks reminded me when we were going back and forth about the project deadline," Richard said to Clay.

Richard's secretary, Marisol Ortiz, was the one who kept the office together. She was a Puerto-Crucian in her early thirties. Her family, though from Puerto Rico, had been in St. Croix for generations. She was no-nonsense and came on board after Richard took over *Fenley and Fenley*. The Fenleys had worked for years with their secretary, Clara, who had decided to retire when the father/son team sold the company. Clara was in her late fifties, extremely nosy and smoked heavily. Richard wasn't disappointed when she announced her imminent departure. It spared him the trouble of asking her to leave.

Marisol was as territorial as a pit bull. She didn't care much about what was happening in anyone's personal life, and Richard loved that about her. She had enough drama of her own. Just don't mess with her well-organized office. She knew where everything was. There was a carefully chosen spot for every single piece of paper. Richard was convinced that she had OCD, but her meticulous nature worked for him and the company.

Marisol and Clay had their differences. She was competition for Clay, once he stepped into the office. Clay was excellent at managing projects outside, but this office was Marisol's turf. Both Clay and Marisol were aspiring perfectionists, constantly getting on each other's nerves. Richard was the designated referee, although he wasn't quite sure how that designation came to be bestowed upon him.

"Mami," Clay blurted, "Richard needs you to confirm two for the *Banks and Cohen* office party." Clay delivered the boss' instructions as he skirted past Marisol's desk.

Clay knew that calling Marisol "Mami" would irritate her no end, so he said it while quickly escaping through the front door. He was already out in the parking lot, opening his truck door before Marisol could respond.

She screamed something at him in Spanish as she stood in the doorway of the office, but the tinted windows in his truck cab were up and his little world was airtight.

He chuckled.

As soon as Kayla stepped into the cafeteria on her third day of work, Mrs. Merchant handed her a form. "Your mom called me this morning and asked me to give you this." Her boss quickly handed her a double-sided financial aid form and smiled.

Kayla couldn't help glancing at the clock on the wall. How had her mother already managed to communicate with Mrs. Merchant? It was barely eight o'clock in the morning. "Thank you, Mrs. Merchant, so how do I get started with the course?" Kayla asked as she accepted the two-sided form from her new boss.

"This is the course form you'll need to fill out." Mrs. Merchant handed Kayla another form and began with the instructions. "There is class at one-thirty this afternoon. All day classes start at that time and finish at five-thirty. You'll report to work here every morning, get a thirty-minute lunch break and then be in class for the rest of the afternoon. I've already spoken to a few people. You are expected to be in class today." With that, Mrs. Merchant left Kayla standing in the cafeteria.

Things were moving a lot faster than Kayla wanted. She really would have preferred to think about this and make her own decision. However, her books were promptly delivered to the kitchen in a recyclable bag by this exceedingly thin guy who had obviously struggled with the package all the way from Mrs. Merchant's office. There was no time to think.

"These are for you..." he panted, "...from Mrs. Merchant," he continued, trying to catch his breath as he wiped the sweat off of his red, pimpled face using the back of his shirt sleeve.

"Thanks," Kayla said to the scraggy messenger.

At exactly one-thirty Kayla headed to Meeting Room B. There were about twenty students waiting patiently for the arrival of the instructor. Most of the seats were already filled. Kayla discreetly scanned the room for any familiar face. There was none. Then, a short Filipino lady came through the door and stood in front of the class. She began with greetings and announced that there was a new student. Looking Kayla in the eyes she said, "Please stand up and say your name and your present job at the hospital."

"Kayla Jackson. I work in the cafeteria."

"Welcome, Kayla. My name is Analyn Ocampo. I am your instructor for this part of the course. You may call me Nurse Analyn or Nurse Ocampo. It really doesn't matter to me. Here is your student handbook." Nurse Analyn walked over to Kayla and placed the publication on her desk. "Please read it very carefully. This information was reviewed in class last week. If you have any questions, feel free to approach me."

Kayla looked at the book in front of her. It read *John F. Luis Hospital License Practical Nursing Program.*

Kayla knew her life was about to change.

CHAPTER 9

It was Friday night and Richard was not looking forward to hanging out with a bunch of acquaintances. Attending the *Banks and Cohen* office party was for business purposes only. For Richard, schmoozing with clients was part of the job. That's how he got more projects. He would have preferred to stay home to tackle one of the two rooms that still needed some work.

The house was a bargain. The previous owners sold it at a good price, but there was a lot of work to be done. It had sustained damage from hurricane Maria. That monster hit the island, packing one hundred and seventy-five-miles-per-hour winds, and higher gusts. It was brutal. It would take the island years to recover. The owners gladly collected the insurance money and bailed.

Richard could see that the structure of the house was still good. He loved the spectacular view, and the price was right. The engineer in him saw it as an investment. He had already completely renovated the kitchen, living, and dining areas. One of the bedrooms he converted into a master suite. That room had a breathtaking view of the Caribbean Sea, and he loved waking up in the morning and being greeted by infinity.

After showering and misting on his favorite cologne "Versace Pour Homme"™, Richard rummaged through his closet for something between casual and semi-formal, if there was such a thing. In his opinion it was a nice pair of dark blue jeans, a white long-sleeved shirt, and a khaki blazer. He put on his favorite pair of Santa Cruz Crocs™ and was out the door.

The parking lot of the Galley was not as full as usual. Tonight there was a private affair for special guests. The space was reserved by the Law Firm of Banks and Cohen.

When Richard entered, it was obvious that the space was set up especially for this event. There were colorful lights in the trees and glowing paper lanterns hanging strategically from the branches. There was live music in the courtyard, a trio. The vocalist was a tall, thin woman with a sultry voice singing "Many Rivers to Cross" by Jimmy Cliff. Her head was wrapped in a colorful turban, and she was wearing a loose African print jumpsuit. One guy was on the keyboard and another was playing bass. *This trio is kickin it,* Richard thought.

Wine was flowing while hors d'oeuvres were presented on silver platters by waiters and waitresses dressed in white shirts and black pants. Richard scanned the crowd. He was already acquainted with some of the staff. Site visits to the new office building had brought him in contact with junior lawyers, the office manager and a few secretaries. He was also looking for Clay who, surprisingly, was not around even though he was usually on time for everything.

"Would you be interested in some caviar, sir?" A shiny silver tray appeared in front of him. The waitress was a curly brunette with naturally pink lips which she pursed as she spoke.

"No thanks, but I would love to have some wine--Pinot Blanc, if possible."

"I can arrange that for you, Sir."

Out of the corner of his eye, Richard spotted Clay speaking excitedly with two of the secretaries who appeared to be enjoying the conversation. It amazed Richard that no matter where they went, Clay could always find at least one acquaintance. The two made eye contact, and Clay eventually excused himself when he realized that Richard was standing alone.

"What's up, man?" They bumped fists. "I see you made it," Clay said, looking at Richard and shaking his head.

"Of course. You didn't expect me to show up?" Richard half-smiled.

"I know you would have preferred to stay home to work on your house." Clay sipped on the beverage he had been holding for quite some time in his hand. Richard suspected that it was a mixed drink. Most likely a mojito.

Richard creased his brow. He knew that Clay prided himself in thinking that he always knew exactly what was on Richard's mind. Admittedly, tonight he was right.

"Hey, Richard," Mark Cohen roared as he descended upon the two men. "Project is coming along nicely. Everyone is impressed with the finishes. Clay you're really pushing it. Thanks."

"That's what I do best, Mr. Cohen." Clay took a slight bow.

"Hi Mark. Nice party," Richard said looking around at the scene admiringly.

Mark Cohen was of average height, a stout white guy originally from Brooklyn, New York. His accent was distinguishable. A receding hairline and thinning hair did not stop him from wearing his almost totally gray bristles in a ponytail. On this occasion, he wore khaki slacks and a white linen shirt. His pinstripe Italian suits were reserved for the office and courtroom. *Banks and Cohen* specialized in civil litigation. Jason Banks and Mark Cohen were beasts in the courtroom.

Mark appeared arm in arm with a beautiful young lady. She looked a lot like a runway model. Tall with long dark hair, dark eyes, and very little makeup. Stunning, actually. Barbara Cohen was around somewhere, so Richard knew this couldn't be some mistress glued to Mark's side.

"Meet Jennifer, my daughter," introduced Mark.

Interesting, Richard thought. He remembered Mark speaking about his daughter, but had never met her.

Daughter? Clay thought. He had no clue that Mark had a daughter.

"Nice to meet you," both Richard and Clay said in sync. The two men did not change their facial expressions. Mark Cohen would never figure out what they were thinking. They had both mastered the art of using poker faces. In business meetings, they used them all the time, especially when they were together. In private, they would work out the logistics during heavy deliberations.

"You kids should hang out sometime. Jennifer is here for a few weeks." Mark Cohen winked at Richard.

Poker face. *Kids? Hang out?* Richard thought. He marveled at his client's choice of words. Did he mean like a play date as if they were five-year-olds? "OK. That would be great, Mark," Richard said, trying not to sound as if he was accepting the offer as though it were a business deal. In reality, he was not interested in getting involved with Mark's daughter, no matter how attractive she was. That relationship would become like a transaction, and he didn't need the pressure.

"You know, Jennifer is studying Law at Harvard," Mark announced proudly pushing out his chest and patting his excessively large midriff. "Yep, following in her old man's footsteps. She'll be coming back to take my place. I need a break."

"I'll get your number from Daddy and give you a call," Jennifer said, purring as she eyed Richard.

Poker face. *Assertive,* Richard thought.

Poker face. *The 3 Bs,* went through Clay's mind.

Mark Cohen walked away with his daughter and Richard and Clay kept their poker faces plastered on for the rest of the evening.

Most people enjoyed Friday nights, but Kayla had a lot of catching up to do. She was the last student on the roster and, of course, one week behind in class. She preferred to get studying out of the way before the weekend started. She had a schedule and planned to stick to it. All homework had to be finished on Fridays. Saturdays were for cleaning and washing. Sundays were reserved for the task of preparing her children for school--ironing school uniforms and preparing bags.

"You finished your homework?" Kayla checked, expecting an affirmative answer from both children.

"Did you finish yours?" Samaria sassed.

"Girl, don't play with me. You finish your homework?" Kayla was too exhausted to hop on the merry-go-round with her daughter. Education was the key out of poverty. Margo had drilled that home time and time again. Kayla ignored the advice, and she didn't want her children to follow her example.

"Yes, I did, and my teacher wants to see you," Samaria reported to her mother.

"Where's the note?" asked Kayla sternly and then half-smiled.

"Right here," Samaria said handing her mother a folded piece of paper.

"Oh, yes. The Parent Teacher Meeting. I forgot all about this," Kayla muttered taking the note.

She typed "PTA meeting" into her phone's calendar.

CHAPTER 10

Six weeks ago, Kayla would never have imagined she would really get the hang of working in the kitchen. Now, she walked into the cafeteria proudly at exactly eight o'clock every morning. It was early for Kayla, but some staff like Shameka was there long before six. So while Kayla was warming up to a new day, Shameka was already roaring and ready to go.

"Girl you are killing that twist out!" Shameka squawked running her fingers through Kayla's hair. "How you get your hair to hold like that and stay so shiny?" she pried.

"I don't do anything special," Kayla said, downplaying her routine and trying to prevent a barrage of questions. "Water and gel, that's it," she shared, moving her head away from Shameka's grubby, thin fingers, trusting there would be no more handling of her tresses.

Pedro was still her drill sergeant, but Kayla was up to the challenge.

"Bring it, girl," she kept saying to herself.

She could tell that Pedro was impressed with her ability to catch on so quickly. He kept pushing her to learn more, and now he was actually commending her. One day after she had finished cleaning the dining area, refilling the drink station, and washing the dishes, Pedro smiled, put his hands on his hips and told her not to worry about the floors. And when he first tasted her Chicken Alfredo, he gave it a big thumbs up.

"Is that a smile I see, Pedro?" she asked.

"Mira muchacha, hazme el favor!" he said. But Pedro was totally blown away.

"OK. I'll give you a break," Kayla said with a wide grin.

Mrs. Merchant showed up after the introductory six weeks had passed and explained that Kayla would have a new assignment. "I'd like for you to be trained as a Ward Assistant."

"I would like that very much, Mrs. Merchant," Kayla said although she didn't have the faintest idea of what the duties of a ward assistant might be.

"Our ward assistants provide food and drink to patients in the morning and afternoon. They also help patients choose and order meals from the menu; and then serve the meals to the patients."

"That sounds interesting." Kayla had been observing another set of staff back and forth in the kitchen stacking trays of food in carts and whisking them away. She figured they must have been delivering food to the patients on various wards. Now she knew what they were called.

"You'll be given a new uniform, of course."

Kayla smiled. "Great." Ward Assistants wore mustard colored uniforms with loose top and bottoms. Under normal circumstances Kayla would cringe at the idea of wearing such an unflattering ensemble, but now she welcomed the idea. The hideous uniform would mark another step closer to her goal.

"It will be good for you to get some experience working with patients since you are taking the LPN course. This is one way we care for our patients' needs, and you should be part of it."

Kayla had reviewed the LPN handbook at home the same day that she received it.

"How is it?" she remembered her mother asking.

"This is some serious stuff, Mommy," she said, putting her palms to her forehead and sighing. "Maslow's Hierarchy of Basic Human Needs" stuck in her mind. Intense studying like this felt so weird. Her head was spinning with all the new information. Loads of processes, principles, ethics, values, safety guidelines...and that was only Nursing 101.

How would she remember it all? It was consuming her. Every so often, she had to take a break and think about something else. Lately, her mind was fixated on seeing her brother, Mally. He was coming to visit soon for spring break, and she couldn't wait to spend time with him.

Kayla's phone beeped and jolted her back to her conversation with Mrs. Merchant. "Please follow me," Mrs. Merchant said.

Kayla peeked at her phone as she followed Mrs. Merchant to another office. "PTA meeting" had popped up. *That's tomorrow,* Kayla thought.

They entered the door marked "HR-2". Like HR-1, the room was a tight fit and bland. Another young lady was there waiting to train Kayla as the new recruit. Damaris Ayala had been working at the hospital for three years. She had also started off in the cafeteria. Kayla recognized her. Damaris was also taking the LPN course. She handed Kayla another book, and a new set of training began.

⁓⁓⁓⁓⁓

"Hey Richard," purred the voice on the other line. "What are you up to?"

Richard immediately recognized the caller, but couldn't remember the name.

"It's Jennifer," she revealed perceptively.

"Hey, what's up..., Jen--Jennifer?" he stuttered, glad for the heads up.

"I'm OK, thinking about you." She continued undeterred.

Why did it seem to Richard like this lady had a plan? *Or was it her father with the plan,* he wondered. *Definitely assertive,* ran through his mind. "Really? Not sure if that's good or bad?" he said and chuckled.

"Yep," she responded, ignoring his sarcasm. "So what are you doing this Friday?"

Another sacred Friday night was on the verge of being hijacked. *Seriously,* he thought. Richard had been mentally prepared to tackle the room he had been working on for the past six weeks. "Incredible!" he grumbled and ran his hand through his hair as he stared blankly out the window. *Why was this project taking so long?* First, he needed to get the bins. Then, he was working overtime to meet deadlines. Next, it was the Banks and Cohen party, and now, this. He wanted to say "No, no", but then there would be the other question--"When?" Richard would have loved to assign this task to one of his employees. Clay was out of the question, of course. He was a retired womanizer and about to marry the girl of his dreams. He had already made it clear to Richard that he would allow no one to disturb that relationship. "What do you have in mind?" Richard pinched his nose.

"I hear that Christiansted is having Jump Up on Friday. You want to go?" she cooed

"Yes. OK. That should be fun," Richard said shaking his head with his eyes closed, happy this wasn't FaceTime.

Richard started thinking to himself: Had Mark Cohen been planning this introduction ever since he first met Richard at a meeting in the Fenley and Fenley office years ago? Brad Fenley did say that Mark admired Richard for being a top-notch engineer that was smart and driven. Mark even said that Richard was ready to take over the world--well, the engineering world in the islands, that is. There were a lot of major projects coming on stream, and it was true that Fenley and Fenley was always in everyone's sights.

"Great! I'll call you to finalize. Take care." She hung up.

Richard stared at the phone in his hand, barely managing to restrain the urge to throw it against the wall. But he had paid too much money for his iPhone X™ to even consider that as a possibility. More than that, the phone was merely the instrument used to facilitate the conversation. So then, he wanted to strangle the conversation. "Calm down, calm down!" he said to himself not noticing that Clay was standing at the entrance to his office.

Clay walked into the office and saw that Richard was clearly disturbed. He looked at his boss and wondered what or who had upset him. As far as he could tell, the projects were all back on schedule. There was nothing outstanding that Clay could think of. "What's up Boss?" Clay asked Richard.

"Hey Clay," Richard mumbled raising his head from its burial place in the palms of his hands, one of which was still clutching the phone tightly. "I'm OK, man."

"Really? So why you look like that?" Clay sat down in one of the chairs in front of Richard's desk still eyeing his boss.

"That was Jennifer," Richard said.

"Mark Cohen's daughter?" Clay asked, leaning forward with raised brows still gazing at his boss.

"That's the one!" Richard made a funny face and shook his head.

"So what's the problem?" Clay asked, creasing his brows.

"She wants to go out this Friday," Richard said and then exhaled. The short conversation he had with Jennifer completely drained him.

"And that's what you're fretting about?" Clay was bewildered at his boss' reaction to the prospect of a date with a beautiful young lady. "Most men would jump at the chance. You, on the other hand, see it as an annoyance. Crazy!"

"I need to work on my house, Clay. Ugh...I keep putting it off."

"Well, do it on Saturday." Clay said, eyeing his boss in amazement.

"That's not an option. Remember I volunteer Saturdays at the youth center. You know...with Jamal. I was thinking that if I start on Friday, I can finish up on Sunday. That would leave Saturday for me and Jamal to hang out."

Fenley and Fenley had adopted Jamal Smith, a thirteen-year-old young man with a dysfunctional home life. Both Clay and Richard took turns mentoring. As a mentor, they were supposed to spend time with a youth, showing interest, teaching new things, and going on outings.

Jamal's mother was a drug addict and his father was in jail for drug trafficking. Jamal wasn't sure when he would ever really know his mother or even see his father again. At the age of thirteen, he had learned to take life as it came.

"Obviously, you got some serious problems on your hands," Clay snickered and rolled his eyes in disbelief. "What could be so bad about hanging out with the Cohen Cover Girl on a Friday night? You amaze me sometimes. Our views on relationships are so different. You know that?"

Just then, a light bulb went on in Richard's head. "Hey, why don't you and Adrianna come with us? We'll make it a double date thingy." For some reason, as beautiful as Jennifer Cohen was, Richard was afraid of being alone with her. She was a little too pushy for his liking.

"OK cool," Clay agreed. He had already planned to spend Friday night with Adrianna and her family. That was the 'lime' on the weekends. He loved going there and hanging out with her father and brothers playing dominoes on the porch. Her mother's cooking was also another tempting incentive. "Where you all planning to go?"

"She wants to go to Jump Up." Richard sulked in his chair like a five year old who was being forced to play with the new kid in the neighborhood.

"OK. We'll meet you all there around eight o'clock." Clay was cool with that. He'll spend a few hours with Adrianna's family and then they would head to Christiansted. His boss needed him, again.

CHAPTER 11

Spring break finally came and Malik was back in St. Croix.

"Malik, you brought the whole of Massachusetts with you," Margo said as they pulled three heavy bags into the apartment. She hadn't realized there was so much luggage until Malik started unloading them in the parking lot outside the building. Margo was so excited and happy to see him that she wouldn't have noticed if he had stuffed an elephant into the trunk of her car.

"Got to treat my peeps right. I have something for everybody. Even for Ms. Bishop in the office." Malik gleamed. He would show the office manager that Malik Jackson was making something of himself.

When Adjoni and Samaria heard the voices, they ran out from their bedroom screaming. "Uncle Mally, Uncle Mally!" The two little voices in chorus were deafening.

Kayla came running too, but she had to wait her turn. Her kids were hanging all over her brother. When all the commotion subsided, Kayla would get her hug. Mally meant a lot to her-- to all of them. He could have been one of those guys sitting on the steps outside the building, but Margo wasn't having it, and Mally had listened. He was her hero.

"Hey, Sis," Malik said and smiled at Kayla.

"Hi big brother."

They hugged and then sat on the couch and faced each other.

"You look more beautiful than when I last saw you." Malik looked tenderly at his younger sister's gleaming face. Passing Omari on the steps a while ago and now seeing Kayla brought back so many memories. He had tried to warn Kayla about Omari as soon as he saw their friendship starting to sprout. But she wouldn't listen.

"We just friends, Mally," she told him.

Things started off like a seed germinating, with Omari giving her candies, little gifts and special "hellos".

"This look more than 'just friends', Kay," he told her.

Then, the relationship began to grow as they walked home from school every day and started spending excessive amounts of time together. Then there was reproduction--Samaria.

"I have nothing to say, Kayla," he told her, swallowing the lump in his throat.

Then, there was Adjoni. There was no pollination; no spreading of the seeds. Neither had anything to offer the other. Understandably, the relationship dried up.

"And you look more handsome than ever." Kayla smiled back admiringly at her brother. "I'm sure you are killing it up there with all those Stateside girls, huh."

"He had better be concentrating on his school work," Margo shouted from the kitchen, "or I will fly up there to Cambridge and fix him."

Malik knew full well that he couldn't mess up. His mother didn't play when it came to their education, and he didn't want any trouble from her.

"Don't worry, Mom. I'm good. I'm concentrating on my *school work*." "School work" reminded him of elementary school, but he needed to reassure his mother.

Kayla had always looked up to her brother. Sure, he had made some stupid decisions like most kids. But she still saw him as steady and focused--nothing like her. For the most part, he always tried to be obedient, again, nothing like her. Apparently, it really worked for him. She always saw him busy with school work or bagging at the Cash and Carry close to their home. Kayla adored him.

"So tell me," he said, looking at Kayla's youthful face and into her eyes—mature eyes that told the whole story of her full life. "What's up with you?"

"Well, I'm working at the hospital now," Kayla said proudly. She was happy that she was starting to enjoy economic independence.

"Mommy told me that you're doing an LPN course too." Mally smiled.

"Yes. It's a lot of studying," Kayla admitted shyly. This was her big brother, Mally, talking to her. Finally, proud of a decision she had made.

"My sister, the nurse, you go girl." He high-fived her. "You are going to be a good nurse too."

"How do you know that?" Kayla asked seeking further validation from her brother. She was enjoying all of the admiration he was pouring on her.

"Kayla, you were always trying to take care of somebody, even animals. Remember the time you brought home that stray kitten and kept it in a cardboard box on the porch. No matter what Mommy told you about diseases from animals, you refused to take it back outside."

"We had Marty for fifteen years. Ate all the rats that ran around this building," Kayla winked at her brother.

"Unfortunately, not the two-legged kind." Both of them cracked up laughing.

"And look at how you take care of your kids," he continued. "They are beautiful. Samaria is going to be a knock out just like you."

"This is a nice bracelet," Kayla screeched, changing the subject. The thick, smooth silver Crucian Hook™ bracelet on her brother's powerful wrist was hard to miss.

"A gift from Elena," Malik said blushing. He touched the bracelet gently and stared at his gift with a twinkle in his eyes.

"Elena Benham?" Kayla shrilled. "I always knew there was something between you two." She waved her index finger at her brother. "You been talking?"

"We just friends." Malik brushed off.

"What's it with guys and 'we just friends'?" Kayla marveled at her brother's dismissiveness. "Come on, Mally, don't tell me you couldn't tell that Elena has been into you forever. Since we were kids."

"Speaking of rats...," Malik said, changing the subject,"... I see your boy Omari still guarding the building from his vantage point on the steps." Malik grinned.

"Omari. Hmph! You know Tamara is pregnant by him now, right?" Kayla cut her eyes and tightened her lips. She wasn't sure if it was out of jealousy because Omari was with another girl or annoyance at the fact that her kids would now be competing for less of the nothing they were already getting.

"No, didn't know. He must have some real good lyrics. Maybe I should get him to give me a few classes," Mally said, chuckling.

"You don't need no classes from that bwoy," Margo screamed from the kitchen.

Mally pushed his lips in the direction of his mother and poked Kayla. The two burst out laughing.

"Hey, I hear tomorrow there is Jump Up in Christiansted. I have some friends playing in the band. Let's go," Malik encouraged. "I need to see some people."

The Crucian Jump Up was a nighttime event when all the stores would be open after hours, sporting sale signs. There would be people crawling all over like ants. Street vendors would come out in their numbers, parking their colorful little carts on the side of the street.

But what Malik was really looking forward to was the serious music that would be pumping from the band.

"Friday? I study on Fridays," Kayla said copping out. "I have a test coming up, and I'm trying not to fall behind. I want to ace it."

"I'll help you study tonight, and we'll go out tomorrow. You need to take a break too," Malik insisted. "Your big bro is in town, girl."

Margo looked over from the kitchen through the overhead cabinets that separated the small galley kitchen from the living area. She was going to say, "Don't come here distracting Kayla from her school work." But instead she said, "Of course you should go, Kayla. You need to get out and have some fun."

This was the first time in a long time that Margo had seen Kayla's face beaming with so much excitement. Besides, Mally wasn't here all the time. It would be good for Kayla to spend time with her older brother. She needed it.

"You too, Mommy. We all going," Malik declared, which was followed by loud cheers from his biggest fans--his niece and nephew.

"Bwoy, but I ain't got nothing to wear," Margo admitted to her son.

"I knew you would say that. Look in that suitcase over there." He pointed to one of the heavy bags. "I brought a few things."

CHAPTER 12

Christiansted was the town that always dared to host Jump Up a few times a year. Christiansted was just as picturesque as Frederiksted. Both towns were situated right on the water--Christiansted to the east of the island and Frederiksted to the west, each with its own fortress built by the Danes centuries ago to protect the island. Brightly painted buildings reflecting Danish architecture dominated both townscapes. It was just that the former exuded a different energy than the latter.

Mocko Jumbies were dancing in the streets to music from a steel pan band. The mood enchanted everyone. Locals and tourists mingled. All the streets were open for foot traffic only. Vehicular parking was kept far away.

Jennifer Cohen, Mark's beloved daughter, was hoping to ride with Richard, but he wasn't too keen on having her as a passenger. Instead, he gladly suggested they meet at the *Banks and Cohen* parking lot and then they would walk over to Strand Street where most of the action was. Clay parked in the *Fenley and Fenley* parking lot which was further away on Hill Street, but would make it easier to get in and out of town with all the traffic. The two met Richard and Jennifer on the corner of West and King Streets. Introductions were made and then, the four started the long walk along King Street and then down towards Strands Street.

Clay and Adrianna walked in front, giving Richard and Jennifer their space. Jennifer was thrilled. *Finally some alone time with Richard,* she thought. Her father had spoken a whole lot about this man, and she was turned on.

The questions began rippling through the air. It was open fire. "So, how long have you been an engineer?" Jennifer shot.

"Almost seven years," Richard answered.

"How long have you owned *Fenley and Fenley*? Do you plan to grow the business?"

"About two years, and I have no idea," Richard reported, starting to resent the direction the conversation was heading.

"Do you plan to stay here in St. Croix? I mean do you like it here?"

"Yes, I love it here. A lot less stress than what I had to deal with before."

"Where are you from, again?" The assault continued.

"Davenport, Iowa."

It seemed as if the battery of questions was never going to end, so Richard started shelling out some questions of his own. "So, what made you decide to go to law school?" he started.

"That was Daddy's dream for me ever since I was a little girl."

"And what was your dream?" Richard coaxed.

"I don't know. I guess the same thing."

"Do you really want to take over your father's law firm?"

"Daddy needs me to do that for him, so I'm willing."

Richard retreated. The inquisition had revealed just what he had predicted. Jennifer was very smart and driven, but her Daddy was everything. Any relationship with Mark Cohen's daughter would be like striking a business deal with Mark Cohen himself. Mark Cohen decided what his daughter should become. Mark Cohen decided where she would go to school. Mark Cohen determined where she would work for the rest of her life. And Mark Cohen would decide who she would marry. Richard did not want to marry Mark Cohen.

He decided to let Jennifer fire away with as many questions as she wanted, and he answered them as best he could. As far as Richard was concerned, however, the battle was over. He disengaged himself from any possibility of dating her. In his mind, this operation was pointless.

The four decided to stop by a store on Strands Street that made hand-crafted jewelry. Adrianna and Jennifer were oohing and aahing over the jewelry in the display window, and inevitably were drawn inside to see what else was for sale. The guys remained outside watching people pass by and speculating on the upcoming basketball playoffs. Which team would eventually make it was always debatable, and both were masters at debating.

Richard was just about to give his opinion on one of the players on the Golden State Warriors™ when he saw a familiar face and figure gliding towards them on the narrow, crowded street. He looked again, harder, focusing his gaze. There she was--hair up in a messy bun this time and wearing a strapless jumpsuit that had a bright coral fitted top and a pair of black and white striped culotte pants.

He eyed Clay. Clay looked at Richard. *Great!* Richard thought. So, Clay had seen her too.

Richard wasn't about to make it an issue. Close by were her kids and a mature woman. *Probably her mother,* Richard presumed. A young man was also part of the entourage, and he had his arms around her shoulders. The guy was nice looking, tall and buffed-- definitely gyming. *Baby Daddy? For one child or both?* Richard wondered.

Out of nowhere, a warm tingling feeling engulfed Richard's body. He was in the fifth grade the last time this kind of feeling crept up on him. His teacher, Mrs. Carter, had asked him to take the desk behind Kathy Harper. The blood had rushed through his body and ended up in all the right places. Although Richard never admitted it then and would never admit it now, he had been smitten.

"Jump Up is tight," Malik said, looking around. "Aren't you glad you came?" He hugged his sister tighter with one arm and locked his other arm with his mother's.

"It's lit, that's for sure," Kayla said smiling, happy to have her brother close by.

The family lingered for a while speaking to some acquaintances as they stood in front of the store where Richard and Clay were waiting. They were all talking to each other while Kayla surveyed the scene. *Did she see me?* Richard wondered. He was sure she had seen him. He sheepishly peeped over at Clay again who was already staring at him. Just then, their dates came out of the store with little blue bags. Poker faces. They collectively decided to move on.

The vibe at Jump Up was just what Kayla needed-- especially the Johnny Cakes from Mr. and Mrs. Thomas, her favorite street vendors. Although she preferred the meatiness of Cavalli, the Thomases knew how to prepare fried Kingfish and Johnny Cakes that were always on point. Kayla had these two local delicacies on her mind as soon as Mally suggested that they all come to Jump Up. The night would not be the same without stopping by the colorfully decorated cart to satisfy her craving.

"Eh eh, look who just show up, Joe," Mrs. Thomas shouted over the loud music as Kayla appeared in front of the cart. And she excitedly waved her hands to get her husband's attention as he fanned the charcoal that kept the oil in his frying pan piping hot.

"You know I'm addicted to your fried fish and Johnny Cakes, so don't act so surprised, Mrs. T," Kayla said. "If you're in the area, you know I'm coming to pay you a visit."

"How you doing, darling?" Mr. Thomas asked Kayla as he came around the cart with outstretched arms prepared to give the warmest hug. "Sara, make sure you throw in a few extra for our favorite customer."

"Of course," Mrs. Thomas said and handed Kayla an oil-stained brown paper bag full of fried fish and Johnny Cakes. "Where the kids deh, Kayla?" she asked.

"Over there with Mommy and Mally, looking at the Mocko Jumbies dance," Kayla said, pointing at her kids. Samaria and Adjoni's heads were cocked back as far as they could go, obviously mesmerized by the extreme height of the dancers with their colorful costumes adorned with ribbons and feathered headdresses.

"Mally here?" Mrs. Thomas exclaimed. "Oh, he's back. Tell him come see me before he leave this place."

"Don't worry he'll come see you, Mrs. T," Kayla said, starting to dig into a piece of fried fish. "Mmm. This is delicious, as usual Mr. and Mrs. T." The music suited the flavor of the fish, and Kayla started dancing as she stood by the cart.

Finally chilling, she thought.

Richard glanced over at the colorful cart across the street where Kayla was dancing alone. She had a natural rhythm that fascinated him. He tried desperately to resist the urge to cross over, but he felt as if the winds were steering him in her direction.

Eventually, Richard gave in to the flow of nature and said to his posse, "I'll be right back." He left Jennifer standing on the sidewalk, talking with Clay and Adrianna in front of a clothing store and strolled across the street.

As Richard got closer, he recognized the sweet scent of juicy berries floating around Kayla, and his mouth watered. The fragrance reminded him of the Summer Sangria Berry Crumble that kept him going back to a cozy little bakery in Davenport.

"The kidnapper making her rounds, I see." Richard said, hoping she would hear him over the loud steel pan music.

Kayla picked up a musky citrusy/floral scent and looked around. It was the guy from Paradise Mart again. She remembered that he had already called her a kidnapper when they spoke in the cafeteria at the hospital. "You don't look like you mind being held hostage," Kayla said and snickered. "I saw you wrapped up a few minutes ago." She looked Richard in the eyes.

He knew it! She did spot him standing outside the jewelry store on Strands Street.

"Wrapped up? I'm just here hanging out with a few friends." Richard said, raising his left palm at her as a sign of honesty.

"Two friends and one kidnapper." Kayla threw out, raising a brow.

"You're too much. You know that?" Richard shook his head and smiled at her.

Just then, the band struck up Pressure's song "Virgin Islands Nice", and the crowd went crazy. People started dancing and scanting in front of the cart, pushing Richard and Kayla over on the sidewalk and blocking the way between the cart and the shop where the rest of Richard's group was waiting.

Kayla smiled. "So, did you patronize any of the shops?" She was now shouting over the music.

"Nah. Didn't really come to shop."

"So, why did you come?"

"Cause I knew you would be here," Richard said and winked at her.

She smiled. "You got jokes, huh." She was blushing, and it made her feel silly because he was obviously hanging out with someone, even if he claimed that this *someone* was only a friend.

"So what do you have in the bag?"

"Fried fish and Johnny Cakes. You should buy some and try it?"

"So, you don't share?"

"Not my fried fish and Johnny Cakes from Mr. and Mrs. Thomas."

Clay couldn't understand why Richard had developed a sudden hankering for something from a food cart across the street until the crowded street cleared a bit and he observed the banter.

It was that Paradise Mart girl again.

Of course, he thought. "This dude 'bout to get us killed?" Clay grumbled under his breath. "The girl walking around with a man, and he still trying to make moves anyway."

"What you say?" asked Adrianna.

"Nothing baby. I'll be right back." Clay dashed across the street, weaving his way through the crowd determined to break up the powwow between Richard and this girl. As he approached the cart where the two were standing, the tall guy emerged. Clay held his breath. "We don't need any problems, we don't need any problems," Clay kept saying to himself. He saw the guy hug the vendors and then his arms went around Kayla's shoulders.

"This is my brother, Mally," Kayla said.

"Malik," Mally said, extending his right hand toward Richard, keeping the introduction formal.

"I'm Richard," Richard said relieved and shook Mally's hand. "Nice to meet you, and this is my partner, Clay." Richard made sure that Clay had gotten his introduction since he seemed so anxious to join the conversation.

"Yes, I'm Clay. Nice to meet you," Clay said, somewhat diffused but still peeved at Richard. No poker face this time. "So what are you getting Richard? You need help carrying anything over?" Clay asked.

Before Richard could come up with an answer, Jennifer had also made her way over to the cart. Richard quickly chose some Johnny Cakes and a few pieces of fried fish.

Poker faces.

"Come on, Kayla," Mally said pulling his sister away. "The guys in the band want to meet you. It was nice meeting you both."

"Same here," Richard said.

Clay nodded in agreement.

"Ah right. See you," Kayla said.

As they strolled away from the cart, Malik started drilling his younger sister. "So who was that guy, Kayla?"

"Just some guy I met at Paradise Mart, Mally." Kayla was doing her best to down-play the *thing* that was clearly happening between her and Richard.

"A lot of chatting for 'just some guy'. You noticed he had a chica linda of his own kind on his arms, right? You saw that she made it over to claim her territory too, right?" Malik lectured.

"Mally, ain't nothing. We met at Paradise Mart, and then I saw him again at work. That's all."

"Just be careful. I ain't want you getting yourself in no trouble. These white people have a lot of power on their side. These man like to play with the pretty faces, but they ain't sticking around. You don't need that in your life, Kaykay."

Kayla exhaled and nodded in agreement.

That night neither Richard nor Kayla could get any sleep.

Mally was right. Kayla didn't need any more trouble in her life. Omari was a chapter in her life she never wanted to repeat. She knew she owed it to herself to listen to her brother this time around and watch herself.

Miles away, Richard lay in his bed, hands behind his head, staring up at the ceiling. This *thing* might get way over his head if he didn't check himself. A young, single mother with two kids must have a lot of baggage. He understood that...intellectually. What he could not understand was why tonight he had felt something for the first time in a very long time, and he just couldn't stop himself from going over to talk to the young lady. Why did he feel as though he was being blown on a bold, yet awkward, path that led to her?

CHAPTER 13

More than a week later at work Kayla read her assignment: Second Floor. Surgical Ward. Room 125. Patient: Annie Duncan. Hernia Operation. Restricted Diet.

With a gentle push of the room door, Kayla was suddenly face-to-face with her first patient. "Good morning, Ms. Duncan. I'm Kayla from the kitchen. I have your breakfast."

"Oh, thank you, honey," Ms. Duncan said. "I am starving. I haven't eaten for over twenty-four hours."

"Let me get the table for you," Kayla said. She had accompanied Damaris a few times to learn the ropes, and now she was on her own. Her job was to deliver the menu and later the food to the patients in Post-Op.

"Can you reach the pillow that's on the floor please? It probably fell while I was sleeping. And I think my painkillers are wearing off. Can you do something about that please?" Ms. Duncan muttered.

"Okay, Ms. Duncan. Let me press the call button for you." Kayla found it amusing that patients viewed her as a nurse assistant. Maybe it was the simple fact that she was wearing a uniform. Whatever it was, she felt proud of herself for the first time in a long time.

"You should think of becoming a nurse yourself," Ms. Duncan managed to say to Kayla through her pain.

Kayla smiled. "I'm working on it."

Annie Duncan was in her late sixties and still very active and adventurous until a strangulated hernia threatened her life. "The doctor told me that I would have to make some changes. This operation was only the beginning."

"So no more heavy lifting," Kayla said.

"That includes my German Rottweiler, Tanga, which I've been raising for five years."

"Oh, I love Rottweilers. How big is she?"

"One hundred and fifty pounds."

"Yes, lifting her would definitely be out of the question."

"It's just that Tanga has been my companion and protector. I can't imagine life without cuddling up with my little pet."

"I guess it would be hard to explain to a powerful beast that lap time is over?"

"Change is not always easy."

"I know what you mean. My brother just visited from Massachusetts. He was here a week ago for spring break, and it was sad to see him go."

"But I'm sure it was nice having him here for a week."

"Yes, it was nice seeing my mother smile again."

"She probably enjoyed watching you two together too. I have three children; so I know how a mother feels."

"Mally is our hero, that's for sure; saying goodbye was hard."

"But life has to get back to normal."

"Well, reality will set in tonight when I sit my first exam for the LPN course."

"You will do fine. I'm sure."

"I'm determined to ace it for Mally," Kayla said and moved to the other side of the bed to let the nurse who answered the call reach the IV pole

"Ms. Duncan, feeling some pain?" The nurse asked, holding a tray of syringes and medication for the IV bag.

"I am."

"Hey Annie," whispered another voice from the entrance to the room. It was a visitor after visiting hours.

"Hey Rich. Found them?" Annie asked her visitor.

"After rummaging through half your house, yes--finally." Richard was Annie's closest neighbor and they looked out for each other. Although, Richard did more looking out for Annie than she did for him. If it wasn't using her spare house key which was in his possession to open her front door because she had locked herself out in a hurry to walk her beloved Tanga, it was going inside to close a window that she had left open before going on vacation.

The latest mission was to find a pair of multi-colored reading glasses and deliver it to the hospital so that Annie could read a few magazines and surf the net while she was laid up for a week in bed. Richard had spent about twenty minutes searching every room in the house and located at least twenty-five pairs of reading glasses, none of which had multi-colored frames. The last resort was the bathroom. There it was, the elusive pair, nicely tucked away in the basket of books beside the toilet.

"You're a lifesaver, Rich. Thanks a million."

"Don't mention." Richard stood at the foot of the bed and looked at the nurse who was staring at him disapprovingly. "Emergency, you know," he said, acknowledging his after hour visit. Then he looked over to the other side of the bed. He saw a familiar face. This one with a hint of wonder. Not disapproval. "Hi. You okay?"

"Yes, I'm fine. Thanks."

"No cafeteria today?"

"No, not today."

Annie looked at Richard. "You know Kayla?"

Richard nodded. "Yes, we've met briefly."

The nurse looked back at Richard and then over at Kayla. *How would this Crucian girl know this stateside man?* She wondered and rolled her eyes. *It could only mean one thing,* she thought. *They say the Caribbean is good for sea, sex, sun, and sand.* "Hmph." The nurse said audibly, then pursed her lips and shook her head.

"It was nice speaking with you, Ms. Duncan. I'll leave you now," Kayla said, easing her way from the side of the bed and towards the door.

"Bye Kayla. Thanks for your help."

"It was a pleasure, Ms. Duncan."

Seeing Kayla again reminded Richard of the conversation he was desperately trying to avoid with Clay. He was expecting Clay to start; he just didn't know when it would happen. He was actually seriously avoiding Clay.

More than a week had already passed by since the episode at Jump Up, and Richard was still trying to pull himself together.

"Why do people climb mountains knowing there is a risk of falling?" he had asked himself as he drove home that night. Now, today at five o'clock in the afternoon he was still wondering why people take risks knowing that there is the possibility of failure. Or why is it that everyday people live in hopes that the unexpected won't happen.

Back in his office, Richard was still trying to regain his composure when his phone rang, jolting him out of his thoughts. It was Clay. "Yeh. Talk to me, Clay," Richard said.

"Hey, Richard, you gotta come down to the hospital. We're about to lay the pipes, but something ain't right. We got to pour the footings tomorrow come what may, so this issue has to be resolved ASAP," explained Clay.

"Did you call Jeff?" Richard asked.

"He's right here, but we need you to come down." Clay sounded desperate.

Jeff was the architect at *Fenley and Fenley*. Cool guy from Texas. Very precise. If there were any problems, Richard knew it could be resolved.

Banks and Cohen site visit flashed up on his laptop screen followed by a loud beep. "I can't come before six this evening, Clay. I have a meeting on-site at *Banks and Cohen*."

"Whenever you can." Clay shook his head. "We're probably going to be here all night anyway."

Richard could hear the disgust in Clay's voice. Another long night. Richard tried avoiding those, but lately, he just couldn't catch a break. He had to meet Jason Banks and Mark Cohen onsite for six o'clock. Hopefully, that meeting would take only an hour, hour and a half--tops. He hoped. Because with those guys he could be there for hours. By eight/eight-thirty he should be at the hospital.

"OK. I'll be there around eight-thirty."

CHAPTER 14

At eight o'clock sharp the test papers were distributed row by row. Kayla's booklet landed on her desk in front of her. She began to slowly scan through the one hundred questions just to prepare her mind. She had been studying for this exam for two whole weeks. Kayla clicked her pen and began. She had two hours, quickly calculating that meant only 1.2 minutes per question.

"Pens down, please," the professor finally announced.

The test was nerve-racking, but Kayla had pushed herself and managed to answer all the questions in time. She would know which ones were right and which were wrong when she got the results. For right now, she just wanted to go home, take a shower and crash in her bed. As she was packing up to leave, her phone vibrated. It was her mother.

"Hey, Mommy," Kayla answered a bit concerned. Her mother usually sent a text message to let her know when they were outside in the parking lot waiting.

"Adjoni came home with a fever today. It finally broke. He's sleeping now, but I don't want to wake him up to take him out in the dew. Can you take the bus home tonight?"

"It's OK, Mom. It's no problem," Kayla said grateful to her mother for being there for her and her children. "Thank you so much, Mommy, for all your help. I love you."

"No problem, dear. I love you too." Margo hung up the phone without hesitation.

There was no doubt that her mother needed some rest too. Kayla could hear the tiredness in her voice. She could never have done all of this without her mother's help. Kayla finished packing her bag and resigned herself to make her way down the long road between the hospital and the Centerline Road. Many of the students had to stay on to work their shifts, and others were going in the opposite direction. No small talk tonight, not even about the exam they had spent two hours sweating over.

Richard had wriggled his way out of a long-winded conversation at the *Banks and Cohen* site. Jason, Mark, and Richard had finished going over the snag list, and he was ready to go. As usual, Mark had a lot more to say. Richard could feel him wanting to broach the Jennifer issue, but that conversation would have to wait for another day.

"Gentlemen, it was nice meeting with you, but I have a fire to put out at the hospital. Please excuse me. I'll have Marisol send the necessary documentation to your office," Richard promised; then he was out of there. He had hoped to be at the hospital by eight, but he drove into the parking lot at about eight-thirty.

"Great! You're here," blurted out Clay, as Richard approached him in the parking lot.

They bumped fists.

"So what's up?" Richard asked, expecting details.

Clay and Jeff began a long explanation about the layout of the building, the direction of the pipes for the plumbing and electrical wiring. Again, Clay reminded everyone that they had to pour the footings early the next morning. They looked at the plans on paper and they looked at what was laid out. They kept comparing the two, going back and forth for about an hour. Everything seemed fine until Richard pulled the measuring tape. It was ten o'clock when they finally found their problem. The backhoe guy, who was fast asleep in his cab because Clay forbade anyone from leaving the site, was off by about five feet. All he had to do was to correct his mistake and then the project would stay on track.

Richard was sure that the guys could handle it from here. "I'm out, Clay." He was hot and tired. He needed to get home, take a shower and hit the sack.

Kayla came out through the automatic doors and headed across the parking lot to the exit. She could see two guys in the distance talking in the lot. *They're really burning the midnight oil on this project,* she thought. *McAllister would be pleased.* She imagined the administrator's tight-lipped facial expression and smiled to herself.

Richard detected the figure hurrying along, and it reminded him of what he saw earlier when he took Annie her pair of glasses. As he walked to his truck, he could see the person more clearly. It looked like Kayla. He wondered why she would be walking down the long road from the hospital so late at night. And why was she no longer working in the cafeteria? Richard jumped into his truck and started his engine. He drove slowly enough to make sure he wasn't mistaken. It was her.

Startled from her thoughts--worrying about Adjoni and concerned about her grade on her first exam--Kayla perceived the hum of a vehicle's engine creeping up closer and closer behind her. She darted towards the exit. Confused, she wondered if she should walk even faster, slow down or go back inside the hospital just in case her life might be in danger. Kayla tensed. The bright headlights got closer, illuminating her path.

This is crazy, she thought.

Kayla decided to stop. She turned toward her pursuer and blinked to adjust her vision. A blue pickup pulled up beside her.

"Do you need a ride?" offered the driver.

Kayla squinted at the driver in the darkness. Why would she even consider taking a ride from a stranger--especially this late at night? But it was a familiar face. It was Richard. She should have known it was a joker, playing around. Waves of conflicting emotions from relief to wariness engulfed her. Mally's words rang in her ears. She understood the words, but then she looked at the long, lonely road ahead of her. A decision had to be made.

"Only to the Centerline, thank you," Kayla said. She couldn't let pride come before her safety. Although, at this point, she wasn't sure which would turn out to be more *dangerous*--walking the lonely road or being a passenger in the truck.

She climbed into the passenger seat and detected a light version of the citrusy, woodsy scent that she had encountered a few times before when he was around. In the cab behind their seats, she spotted rolls of architectural plans, a large, beat-up toolkit, and a black leather backpack--nothing suspicious. Mally would be proud that she had the sense to check.

Richard looked in the rearview mirror, but Clay's back was turned as he talked to the backhoe driver. "So, no more cafeteria?" he asked. He looked at Kayla. She seemed uncomfortable, unlike the night at Jump Up.

"No," Kayla said, trying to keep the conversation short. She found Richard intriguing, but her older brother was of a different opinion.

"Holding hostages in there, huh?" Richard joked, trying to lighten the mood.

Kayla couldn't help but smile. It was obvious to her that this guy couldn't take a hint. "No, I'm taking a nursing course," Kayla revealed, trying to be polite and grateful for the ride.

"So you want to be a nurse, huh?" He smiled at her.

"We'll see," she said, careful not to be too friendly, but it was so hard to control herself.

"So do you speak like this all the time or have you changed your accent because you think I won't understand what you're saying?"

"Meaning?"

"Well, Crucians have their dialect, but yours is not that strong right now. I'm just saying..."

"Oh OK. Didn't notice."

"I'll understand if you speak in your dialect."

"Thanks for letting me know."

"For some reason, we are not supposed to have friendly conversations."

"For some reason?" Kayla asked. *What was this guy talking about?* She looked at Richard out of the corner of her eyes.

"You see...," he said, "...I don't know if you have a bodyguard somewhere around."

"I ain't ge' no bodyguard, but I see you have one though," she blurted in her strong Crucian dialect.

"She is just a friend," Richard said.

"And she know that?" Kayla sucked her teeth.

"Well, I've never said otherwise." Richard looked at Kayla. Their eyes locked like magnets.

Kayla glanced away. The Centerline Road was only a few feet ahead.

"Like that makes a difference?" Kayla said, keeping her eyes straight ahead, dropping her dialect and picking up her partial stateside accent again.

Looking across at his passenger Richard said, "It makes a difference to me,"

"Well, she was sure to mark her territory at Jump Up the other night." Kayla shook her head. *Men are all the same.* "Anyway, I appreciate the ride," she continued.

Richard looked across at her again.

"Really I do," she said as they arrived at the corner of the hospital road and the Centerline. "You can let me off. I can take the bus from here."

"I can take you home if you want. Where do you live?"

"Far from here." Kayla pursed her full lips in no mood to go down the road her brother specifically told her to avoid. Although, deep down inside she felt differently.

Richard stopped the truck. "You don't have to take the bus. Really. I would like to take you home. Who knows, one day you might be my nurse."

Kayla bit her bottom lip and contemplated the offer. She was torn. So far, she hadn't seen any buses passing on the Centerline Road, and there would be another long, isolated road gaping at her once the bus dropped her off at the gas station close to the apartment buildings. She and her mother had already discussed that they would make sure she would never be put into a situation where she would have to walk home on Tuesday nights. On the flip side, Adjoni coming down with a fever was unanticipated. There was no alternative. Kayla would make the sacrifice. Deep down inside, she was drained and not really in the mood to stand on the side of the road in the dark night, waiting to catch a bus that would probably not show up anytime soon; let alone, to make the long trek to the pavilion.

"OK. I live down West. In Frederiksted. In the Walter I.M. Hodge Pavilion," she conceded.

"Is that some sort of villa or something?" Richard asked. "I've never heard of it."

"I'm not surprised." Kayla rolled her eyes and exhaled.

"What's that supposed to mean?" Richard was puzzled at her comment. He wondered what impression she had of him? A Statesider who only mingled with other Statesiders, one who hardly if ever got too close to Crucians? Or, more, a white man who didn't mix with black people at all?

"Well, you usually stay in East End, right?" she smirked.

Richard stared at her in disbelief. "Yes, remember that's where we first met--in the East End?"

Kayla managed a smile.

"So, Paradise Mart in Frederiksted is what you consider East End?" Richard said.

"Anyway..."

They both knew that they had met at the Big Paradise Mart in Frederiksted on the western side of the island.

"Now, who got jokes?" Richard asked.

She was being cynical, and he was on to her. They looked at each other and smiled.

"You win," Kayla said.

The rest of the ride to the pavilion was very pleasant. Introductions were formally made.

"Richard Patterson."

"Kayla Jackson."

"You know Iowa is so different from St. Croix."

"So why did you decide to move here? Most Statesiders can't take the slow pace for too long."

"It was better for my health."

"Really?"

"Yes, the doctor warned me that if I didn't slow down I'd be dead."

"So are you slowing down here?"

"Kind of."

"Picking up a strange woman who you think might have a bodyguard or two and offering to take her home to a place you don't have a clue about isn't exactly what I would call 'slowing down'."

"Well, according to the strange woman that I picked up, there are no bodyguards. So, I shouldn't be worried."

"OK then."

"What I consider stressful is renovating my house," Richard said changing the subject.

"Where? East End, of course."

"Yes, East End. Sorry to disappoint you. That's where I found a house that I liked."

"So how far are the renovations?"

"It's crazy. Every time I think I'm done, something else comes up. I did manage to get a few key areas done."

"Key areas?"

"Yes, the foyer, the living area, the kitchen, and the master bedroom."

"Sounds like you've gotten pretty far," she said chuckling.

"Well, still a long way to go. So what about you?"

"What about me?"

"Why did you decide to study nursing?"

"It's something I've always wanted to do--I guess. Taking care of people is what I like to do."

"And how do you do it with two kids?"

"My mother is a big help. Without her, I couldn't do it."

"So, you only have two kids?"

"What do you mean by 'only'?"

"Sorry, didn't mean it the way it sounded. And your brother? He seems very protective."

"He is a bright spot. I love him bad." Kayla smiled and rambled on about her life with Mally. Not a word about Omari. She even confessed to Richard about how nervous she was taking the LPN course and the dreaded exam that night which she had so thoroughly studied for.

When the gas station on the corner came into view, Kayla instructed Richard to take the dimly lit road straight ahead after the traffic light. Eventually, pale brown buildings came into view. They had finally arrived at the pavilion. The ride was longer than Richard had expected, but the company was pleasant. He felt free to express himself. *How could someone he had just met make him open up like this?* He wondered.

"You can let me off there by the big mahogany tree you see ahead," Kayla said, trying to get Richard to drop her off at the entrance to the parking area for her building.

"What? No. I need to make sure you get in safe and sound," Richard said, insisting on driving right into the parking lot.

"Apparently, chivalry isn't dead," Kayla said under her breath.

Richard pulled into a spot in the poorly-lit parking lot that had seen better days. The asphalt had crumbled to bits from wear and tear and virtually no stripes were visible to mark parking spaces. "Let me at least walk you to the door," he volunteered, unbuckling his seat belt.

"Wait, Richard, please stay in your truck," Kayla begged. "This is a government-owned housing project even if it says *Pavilion* on the sign."

"At least let me wait to make sure you get in okay," Richard said. "I see those guys on the steps over there."

"Listen to me," Kayla said taking control of the situation, "as soon as I get out of this truck, please head out of this parking lot."

"Could I at least call you to make sure you're OK?" Richard asked, hoping he sounded genuinely concerned for her safety.

"Fine!" Kayla mumbled and rattled off her number as he typed it into his contacts. "My number is 254-8827." Then, she jumped out of the truck.

"Which apartment is it anyway?" Richard asked through his lowered window.

"That one right there," Kayla said, pointing to the apartment to the right on the 2nd floor.

The situation felt awkward. Clearly, this man had never been to a pavilion. Because why on earth would he want to get out of his truck to escort her to her apartment? It made no sense. Kayla started feeling like she should never have accepted the ride. What was she thinking risking a stranger's life just to enjoy doorstep service? An outsider in her neighborhood at this time of the night--crazy.

Richard had to admit to himself that he was not at all familiar with neighborhoods like this one. He had grown up in the suburbs of Iowa, Riverview Terrace. Sure, he had been to Brady Village in Davenport during a field trip when they were studying public housing design, but it was nothing like the buildings he saw in front of him at the moment.

The guys on the steps were looking their way.

As Kayla walked towards them, she saw the puzzled looks on their faces. "Good night," she said and maneuvered her way up the steps.

"Check out that sweet-looking, liquid blue Ford F-150 Raptor™ pickup with the wicked rims, mehson," she heard Curtis say.

Kayla could only imagine that at eleven o'clock at night they were anxious to see who the passenger was. Now they knew--it was she, Kayla. The truck was definitely fully-loaded. Curtis, who was also known as "Bulldog", went on to inform the others of all the stats. He knew every detail about any vehicle you could name. He had always dreamed of becoming an automobile designer. Sad to say, his dreams took him no further than the steps outside the pavilion buildings.

"Good night," they all managed to say in unison, still gawking.

Richard drove slowly out of the parking lot, all the while staring in his rearview mirror to make sure Kayla made it safely up the steps past the guys.

Kayla entered the shadowy apartment. All of the lights were off except the one in the hallway. Her mother had fallen asleep on the couch, understandably exhausted. Kayla went over, gave her weary mother a kiss and whispered "Goodnight, Mommy." Then she went into Adjoni's room. He was sleeping soundly without any fever. Her mom had done a wonderful job. As she bent over to kiss her little prince, her phone beeped. A message.

"U OK? It was from Richard.

"Yeh, fine," Kayla typed. "Thanks for ride. Get home safe."

Kayla went into her mom's room and looked out of the northern window. She saw the fiery red glow of the truck's tail lights at the entrance. Richard had stopped there to make sure she had made it in okay.

Richard smiled at Kayla's reply. A delicious fruity sweetness from her perfume lingered in his truck and accompanied him all the way home.

CHAPTER 15

The next day, Richard couldn't resist messaging Kayla first thing in the morning. "Good morning. Ready for class?" His mind had been on this woman before, but now the long drive with her to the pavilion in Frederiksted had whetted his appetite even more.

"Working in the cafeteria now. Will be taking breakfast on the ward soon. Class is this afternoon," Kayla typed in her phone and pressed "send".

"Enjoy your day."

"You too."

Clay walked into Richard's office as Kayla's last text reply came through. Richard was smiling when he looked up at his visitor. Today was going to be the day he and Clay would have the dreaded conversation. In fact, Richard could sense that now would be the time.

"Why do you have that look on your face, man?" Clay asked Richard.

"What look?" Richard kept his head down and began shuffling some papers on his desk.

"A spiritual one. Like you just saw an angel or something. Who was that?" Clay pried. "The Cohen girl?"

"No." Richard knitted his brow.

"Then who? Cause I know it's not business." Clay was anxious to find out who was on the other line. He sat down in front of Richard's desk.

"Just...someone," Richard said.

"Don't tell me you seeing that Paradise Mart chick and ain't come to me for clearance?" Clay's voice was full of resentment. "You tryin' to get with a Crucian girl without asking for my advice, Richard?"

"We're just friends that's all," Richard said, recalling that only last night he had told Kayla the same about Jennifer. This time he may not have been completely honest, but that's all he could say for now.

"Look at me, man. In the eyes. Look at me in the eyes," Clay said. "Let me break it down for you. You are not just friends. You hooked, man, like a junkie on crack. How do you know what she's about? If there are any baby daddies lurking around. The drama is real, Richard. I'm telling you." Clay was adamant.

"Well, she told me..."

"Told you? Told you what?" Clay moved to the edge of his seat and cocked his head to hear Richard's response.

"She told me that there are no bodyguards around." Richard cringed sensing that an attack was imminent.

"Wait, did you all speak again after Jump Up?" Clay moved further to the edge of his seat and looked Richard in the eyes.

"I gave her a ride home last night from the hospital," Richard admitted sheepishly.

Clay's eyes and mouth opened wide. "That's why you were easing your way out of the parking lot?"

"She needed a ride. I couldn't let her walk down that long road--all alone. Come on, man. Cut me some slack, Clay."

"What about the Cohen girl, Jennifer? We had a nice time at Jump Up. She's a little wired, but she and Adrianna hit it off."

"Well, then Adrianna should date her."

"You know what I mean, man."

"We hung out that night. It was all right, but I didn't make any promises." Richard frowned and shook his head.

"You know women, Richard. They don't need promises. They just assume things." Clay chuckled.

"Well, I told her I wasn't ready for that now." Richard rubbed his chin.

"So you made it clear?" Clay gazed at Richard.

"Yes, very clear"

"I got to check out Ms. Paradise Mart for myself to make sure the coast is clear," Clay said. "So, where does this chick live?"

"In some pavilion in Frederiksted," answered Richard, struggling to remember the exact name of the complex where he had given Kayla a ride just the night before. His brain was foggy.

"Pavilion? Like villas or something?" Clay's idea of a pavilion was a condo or townhouse. No matter how many creative names the government tried to put on its housing communities (attempting to improve tenant morale), it was taking a while for Crucians to connect the word pavilion with the projects.

"Walter something." Richard couldn't remember the whole name Kayla had rattled off, nor did he remember to read the sign at the entrance when he took her home.

"Walter I.M Hodge Pavilion?" Clay sought clarification.

"Yes, I think that's it," Richard said. The name sounded familiar. He was pretty sure that was it.

"The projects!" Clay barked. He jumped out of his seat. He knew that the politically correct description was "housing community," but that was beside the point right now. He continued, "Man, you are crazy. You know that? You took her home in the hood at what time? Like almost eleven o'clock at night? In your Raptor™ with the wicked rims? Really, Richard! Man, you are miscalculating--big time."

"Well..." Richard was speechless. Maybe it was a bad move, he thought. But he couldn't stop himself.

"Richard, let me explain something to you," Clay said, taking a deep breath. "My wedding is in three months. I want you to be there. No, I *need* you to be there, but I don't want any shots fired. I want that day to be memorable for all the right reasons."

"Clay, no shots will be fired at your wedding," Richard said, "--at least not because of me."

Clay couldn't breathe. He was now hyperventilating. This *thing* between Richard and this Paradise Mart girl unnerved him. Who was this girl? He had to find out--and soon. Before she showed up again and before Richard ended up dead on a beach somewhere. Clay's mind started racing. He knew a few guys from Frederiksted. He definitely could think of some buddies who would know people in the pavilion. "No more text messages until I report back to you. You check me?" Clay said, trying to make the precariousness clear to his boss.

"Yes. OK," Richard said, trying to figure out what Clay was expecting to find out about Kayla.

"I'm serious, Rich!" Clay said, suddenly sounding like Richard's father. Clay accepted the fact that he had just gotten another project to manage.

CHAPTER 16

It was the month of May, and Kayla had survived her probationary period. She was now considered permanent staff. She felt good to finally be an official JFL Hospital staff member. Mrs. Merchant was the one appointed to deliver the news, of course. Certainly, HR had that responsibility, but Kayla was sure that Mrs. Merchant wouldn't allow anyone else to do the honors. Even Mr. McAllister came by to congratulate Kayla and commend her on her progress.

"Good job, Ms. Jackson!" he said. "Keep up the good work."

For the first time in her life, she had been gainfully employed for more than two months. It was a milestone for her.

One food tray on Kayla's route was marked for the Pediatric Ward in the Neonatal Unit. It was strange because babies don't receive food trays from the kitchen.

Kayla went through the double doors and slowly pushed open the door marked "ICU-Room 1". In the room, she saw a crib with a baby sleeping soundly and a lady sitting in a chair next to the crib. There was no name on the tray, only the room number.

"Hi, my name is Kayla. I brought food from the kitchen." Kayla spoke softly trying not to rouse the sleeping infant.

"Oh, thank you. I'm starving," the lady whispered.

As Kayla rested the tray on the table next to the window, two nurses came in. One was rolling a machine and the other had some instruments stuffed in her pocket. They began probing the little body and writing notes on the chart that was attached to the crib. They changed intravenous fluid bags and gave a few injections. The baby boy, too weak to scream, sobbed in protest. As little and as sick as he was, there was hope in his eyes. With tears rolling down her cheeks his mother held his little hand and whispered reassurances throughout the painful ordeal.

Once their routine was completed, the nurses looked at the mother and nodded. He had made progress. They were finally seeing some light at the end of the tunnel. Relieved, the mother sobbed uncontrollably. It was at that moment Kayla understood that what she was learning as a nurse was not about her at all. She could really make a difference in someone's life. This is what she had always wanted to do with her life. Classes, studying and exams were taking on a life of their own.

"Shameka, why don't you do the LPN course?" Kayla had asked one day.

"Girl, I hate to see blood," Shameka confessed. "If I don't like taking injections, can you imagine me trying to give one to someone? Worse if it's a crying baby."

Shameka and Pedro had completely thawed out.

"Kayla, you can be my private nurse any day," Pedro leered at Kayla, winking his large brown eyes.

Not only was the winking creepy, but a mental picture of trying to turn him over to change his sheets and underpad flashed through her mind. He was a robust guy with hair on every square inch of his body. Kayla could tell that Pedro would be the kind of patient that would make her job very difficult. "Down boy!" Kayla hissed at her supervisor, using a dog trainer's hand signal for controlling their furry clients. She brought her arm straight down pointing to the floor.

Pedro had admitted that he was still living at home with his mother, and even at thirty-eight years of age, he had no intention of changing that. He stated that Mrs. Peguero loved having her son at home with her. They could cook together and complain about every The Price is Right™ contestant that dared to give an incorrect answer to their favorite host Drew Carey. Life was just how Pedro liked it.

Unlike Pedro, who was quite comfortable living in his mother's house in Campo Rico, Kayla dreamed of living in her own home one day. A house with a yard. She had never had one. All her life was spent as a resident of Building 5 Apartment 2B, Walter I. M. Hodge Pavilion, Frederiksted, St. Croix. All of the apartments come with a little porch next to the kitchen that is used for washing and hanging out clothes.

The green space was the grass around the buildings--if there was any left after the kids trampled on it playing ball games. Some tenants bought artificial grass rugs to create green spaces on their porches. Kayla's mother never bothered to do that. She never had time to relax on the porch, anyway. Now, with all that was happening in her life, Kayla was finally beginning to dream again.

Clay decided to start his investigation with Butch, a high school friend. Butch didn't live in the projects, but he sure knew everyone who did. He was six foot six and carried around three hundred and fifty pounds of pure muscle. His present occupation? That was never quite clear to Clay.

"Watch Butch, this your boy, Clay. Wha' you sayin'?" Clay started and cleared his throat. He tried to find the right words to begin explaining the reason for his call to his bro from high school. "I have a partner checking a girl from Sofarelli." Clay wasn't about to say Walter I.M. Hodge Pavilion. All the locals knew the housing community as Sofarelli. Clay continued, "A bombshell...She look sweet, fo' real."

"Two kids?" asked the husky voice.

"Yes, works at the hospital now." Clay gave more details.

"That's Omari's ex," Butch said, "She was his girl for years, but he was going nowhere really fast. He has some other chick now who is pregnant for him."

"So...ex?" Clay wanted to confirm. "And Omari?"

"Harmless dude trying to make it big sitting on some cruddy steps all day," Butch said, cracking up laughing.

"OK, thanks man," Clay said, grateful for the information.

Before Clay could hang up, Butch had one last thing to say. "Hey, Clay. Tell your partner he's not the only one checking that honey, but she's on lockdown. Has been so for years. Doesn't give chances."

"Really?" Clay was speechless.

"Who is your partner anyway?" Butch was curious.

"A dude from Iowa," Clay said, cringing. He waited for a response.

Butch laughed and then got silent for a second, "Well, I ain't know what to say, man. Tell him all kinds have tried. He's gonna need superhuman powers to unlock that safe."

Butch had spoken. He had pitched in his two cents. Clay knew Butch as the guy who was always the bouncer at a party or club. He knew everybody. He had a wicked sense of humor, but one look at him and you knew he could wipe the grin off your face in a minute, literally.

CHAPTER 17

"Yeh, Clay," Richard picked up the call via the Bluetooth™ in his truck.

"We got to talk, man."

"About?"

"Your friend from Paradise Mart."

Now, Richard was nervous. *Did Clay find out something about Kayla that could be a deal-breaker?* He wondered. Richard knew about the kids, he said he didn't want to be burdened with someone else's problem, but for some reason that didn't matter much anymore. "When?" Richard asked. As far as he was concerned, the sooner the better. "I'm heading to the office now."

"I'll meet you there."

When Richard got there, Clay had already entered the building. In fact, he was sitting in Richard's office in a chair right next to his desk.

"This looks serious," Richard muttered staring at Clay.

"You need to sit down," instructed Clay.

He sat on the corner of his desk and bit his lip. "OK. So tell me what you found out."

"How badly do you want to get with this girl?" Clay studied Richard's face.

"I thought this conversation was about the dirt you went to dig up on her." Richard felt the same nervousness he had as a child when he was next in line to suffer the pain of an injection. He was anxious to get the ordeal over with.

"Just answer the question!"

"Well, she seems nice and everything...," Richard paused. "I don't know where we're going to go from here. I'm not sure what you are getting at. I'm confused." He moved from the edge of his desk to his chair.

"I spoke with my boy, Butch. Look, this chick isn't some loose girl from the hood," Clay started.

"Yeh, go on." Richard wanted to hear more. Both elbows were on his desk with interlocking fists supporting his chin.

"Here's the low-down: She has an ex, but he is not dangerous. He's actually with some other girl now. He might even have been one of the guys on the steps when you carried her home. She's not with any dude right now, although, according to Butch a lot have tried. All kinds, he says. Butch says she's on lockdown, and if you want to get with her, you need to say your prayers because you'll need help from a Higher Power. That's it!" wrapped up Clay.

Richard listened carefully to every word that came out of Clay's mouth. He tried to imagine what Butch's words were really saying about Kayla Jackson. He leaned back in his chair and looked up at the ceiling tiles. There was a brown watermark staring back at him.

One he had always promised to take care of. "So what do you think?"

"What do I think?! It's all about you, man. I mean, I believe Butch. There's no doubt. But after hearing this, do you really think you have a chance?" Clay was now himself doubtful.

"I don't know?" Richard blew.

"What do you really want with her?" Clay pushed.

"I'm not sure," Richard vacillated.

"Well, you better be sure, because someone might get hurt. And that someone could be you," Clay spelled out for Richard.

Clay got up and sauntered out of the office. His boss needed some time to digest all of this. Richard heard the usual raillery between Marisol and Clay, and then everything went silent. He was alone with his thoughts.

He was relieved that Clay hadn't brought a stack of copied police records for him to review. Of course, he was happy that she checked out. But Clay's question rang in his ears, "What do you really want with her?" He honestly couldn't say. He just wanted to get to know her for now. What do people really want when they start relationships anyway? Different people want different things--companionship, reassurance, emotional support, financial support. The list could go on and on. What was he looking for? His relationship with Amber tanked. Jennifer Cohen, although strikingly beautiful, made him nervous.

Richard knew that Jennifer and her father, Mark, would never let him be himself. They would try to drive him to the limits. The conversation he and Kayla had the night he carried her home didn't make him feel pressured at all. She was smart. He could see that. Still, she was interested in his thoughts. She would let him speak, and then she asked questions about his feelings. It was amazing. He could have talked to her all night.

Richard picked up his phone. He typed "When can I see you again?" and pressed send.

A few minutes later Richard checked to see if there was a response. There was nothing. Had she already locked him out?

An hour later Richard picked up his phone to check for messages. There was one message. It was Clay reminding him to speak with Jeff about another snag they had at the Diabetes Center.

"OK," he responded.

⁓

The message came through when Kayla's class was just about to start. She had no choice but to respond later. This was all she needed! Now, she wouldn't be able to concentrate in class. She kept thinking about the message and what her answer should be. She was glad that she was in the middle of something. It gave her some time to think. Mally's words rang in her ears.

She had resolved to never get into another relationship like the one she had had with Omari. There were so many promises made to ease the pain of disappointment. She didn't want another baby, another baby daddy. Those were out of the question. What were Richard's intentions? It's always hard to tell in the beginning.

Her class was almost over, and Kayla was still thinking about the best way to respond to the text from Richard.

It was a total blur.

Everything jumbled into one.

Nurse Analyn said, "It is a decision-making process, including both cognitive and activity components."

Kayla heard, "You have to make a decision about this man."

Nurse Anayln continued with, "The whole process is dynamic and interactive since data from one phase can aid in maintaining or altering the other phases."

Kayla heard, "Will you keep interacting with Richard and take it to the next phase and go on a date with him, which could alter your whole life."

It was crazy.

She even forgot that she had gotten a ninety percent on her exam.

As soon as class was over, Kayla lurched out of the hospital building like she had been suffocating. She relished the fresh air. A walk was just the thing she needed to get the blood flowing to her brain. She knew she would have to respond to the text, but it couldn't happen now. She had a gut feeling that the response she chose would change her life forever. Kayla strolled to Centerline Road, caught a bus, rested her head against the window, and closed her eyes. She kept that position all the way down to Frederiksted.

Kayla finally made it home; physically tired and mentally exhausted. Her mom was already home and in the process of cooking dinner. Her kids greeted her cheerfully but were busy watching TV, of course. Their homework was nicely laid out on the dining table for their mother's review as per her instructions. She went to her mom in the kitchen and kissed her on the cheek.

"How was your day, Mommy?" Kayla asked with her arms around her mother's shoulders.

"It was nice and easy, the way I like it," Margo said. "How was yours?"

"Just the opposite, rough and challenging," Kayla chuckled and stared at the message again. "What's you answer going to be?" she whispered to herself.

She limped over to her kids and plunked herself down on the couch between them. Snuggling in closer, they pinned her on both sides. She had grown to love watching Sponge Bob™. Eventually detangling herself, Kayla got up to shower and prepare school bags for the next day. At seven o'clock they ate dinner and at eight-thirty it was time for bed.

Kayla stared at the message again. She replied.

At six-thirty in the evening, Richard picked up his phone to check for messages. One message. It was Jeff asking to meet with him briefly in the morning at nine o'clock.

"No problem," he responded as he laid the phone back down on his kitchen counter.

Richard heard his phone beep again. It was nine-fifteen at night. One message. It was from Kayla.

"Sorry"

He stared at the phone puzzled. *Sorry?* He shook his head.

"What do you have in mind?" Another message appeared.

It took her seven hours and forty-five minutes to respond. Getting to know this girl was going to be tricky, Richard thought. "Was starting to think you didn't want to see me again," Richard typed.

"Got your txt just as class was about to start. Took bus home. Mommy duties. I apologize."

"It's OK, but thanks for the explanation." Richard sensed her exhaustion and tried not to put her under any more pressure.

"So, what do you have in mind?" Kayla repeated.

Richard hadn't thought about anything in particular. He just wanted to see her again. *Where do you carry a girl like this?* He didn't know if he should include her kids or try to meet her alone. He was treading uncharted waters, and he felt confused. Why had he not worked out the logistics before he sent the text? He had had seven hours and forty-five minutes to figure it out, and he couldn't come up with anything.

"Where's your head, Richard?" he scolded himself.

Richard stared at Kayla's question again. "When are you free?" He asked, trying to buy some time.

"Never! I'm a mother." Kayla messaged back quickly.

That was a stupid question, thought Richard. He had to try to think clearly. "Can you find some time on Friday night?" he typed and pressed "send".

"I can ask my mother to babysit."

"I can pick you up at seven," Richard offered.

"I'll meet you at the gas station," Kayla replied.

It was Wednesday. Richard had at least one day to think about where he would take her. An elegant indoor restaurant or an informal beach bar and grill? Or a movie? Or he could whip up a nice dinner for her at his house? *Nah,* he thought, *that would be a little too serious.*

His mind ran on Sunny's Beach Bar deep in the west. It had a nice relaxing ambiance. The scene was casual, right on the beach in Frederiksted; and there was always live music. The food was superb, too. Tables were scattered on the beach strategically nestled between the trees for privacy which made it the ideal spot. It was cozy, but not mushy. Richard didn't want to overdo it. Who knows? This could very well be the first and possibly the last date. There was one thing, though. He began to type another message.

"How do you feel about iguanas, the reptiles?" Richard pressed "send". It was ten o'clock; there was no reply.

CHAPTER 18

The next morning Kayla responded to Richard's question as she sat on the bus on her way to work. "I can't stand lizards, but they're OK as long as they don't get too close."

Richard was already in his office when the text message came through. "Lol," he replied. He was anxious to see Kayla again. This time on a formal date. Neither of them could have imagined that their chance meeting in a department store would evolve into a sort of friendship, let alone an official date that was about to happen in less than twenty-four hours.

"We need your RSVP for the wedding, Richard," Clay said, waltzing into the office unannounced as usual.

Marisol had already promised to lock him out of the building entirely if he kept walking in on her boss like that. As far as she

141

was concerned, it was totally disrespectful of Clay. As far as Clay was concerned, Richard couldn't possibly have any meetings or conversations that he didn't already know about.

"Oh, yes. When is the deadline?" Richard queried. He had completely forgotten about RSVPing.

"Do you have a date?" Clay asked.

"Not sure yet," Richard exhaled.

"Spoke with your Paradise Mart friend lately?" Clay half-smiled, but really wanted to know.

"Yes," Richard said, intent on not divulging too much information.

"So you decided to go for it like a bull to the slaughter, huh." Clay shook his head and chuckled.

"You really got jokes, man. Where do you come up with these things?" Richard marveled at Clay's choice of words.

"How soon can you RSVP? We are trying to finalize the seating," Clay said.

"I'll let you know on Saturday." Richard grinned.

Clay flashed a smile at Richard. They both knew what that meant. Something was definitely going down on Friday. Clay shook his head and walked out of the office.

"An island girl who is afraid of lizards? That's interesting," Richard typed and pressed "send".

"LOL," Kayla typed.

Iguanas were different from the lizards Crucians were used to. The latter were small, green wall climbers that scurried about eating flies and other small insects while trying to avoid human contact. The former had inhabited St. Thomas for years. They were big fellows who had no problem defending themselves against humans. Recently, there had been a surprising increase in the iguana population on St. Croix.

The Wildlife Foundation, sponsored by the government, tried to convince Crucians that one fine day hundreds of iguanas suddenly chose to migrate. How strange that after decades of inhabiting St. Thomas, countless slaughters (group of iguanas) would all decide to make the forty-four mile swim over to St. Croix. Kayla didn't buy it. *Something smells fishy.*

Kayla looked up after sending her message only to meet four gaping eyes. "Kayla, you got a little somethin' somethin' going on?" Shameka giggled.

Shameka and Pedro revealed that for a while they had been noticing something. "That glow!" they both said giggling.

Kayla had not even told her mother about Richard, so she sure wasn't going to volunteer any information to these two. Her story would probably end up on the cover of the *St. Croix Avis.*

"When did sending text messages become a crime?" Kayla jested.

"Since you started talking to someone special," Pedro lashed back. "You should see the smile on your face."

"You two are too much for me. Let me go make my rounds." Kayla covered herself, escaping without any further exchange.

Telling Margo would be the same as telling Mally. Her mother would spill the beans. She knew it, and Kayla wasn't ready for that right now. Mally had his talk with her, and she respected his opinion a lot. Still, deep inside, she felt she had to give this guy a chance. The truth was that Mally didn't know anything about Richard--in fact, neither did she. That being said, Richard had piqued her interest.

Kayla was still trying to figure out an explanation to give her mom for her Friday night outing? She didn't like sneaking behind her mother's back. Been there, done that. If something happened, what would she say? Margo would be devastated. Kayla knew she had to be honest and up front, but she would ask her mother to promise not to tell Mally anything for right now.

After work that evening, Kayla eased into her mother's room where Margo was folding and putting away clothes.

"Mommy, can you please babysit for me on Friday night?" Kayla asked and sat on the bed. Her palms were clammy.

"You goin' out?"

"Yes, someone asked me out on a date." Kayla cleared her throat.

"Someone? Like who?"

Kayla swallowed and looked down at her feet. "Just someone I met at Paradise Mart."

"The white man Mally was talking about in the car?"

"His name is Richard." Kayla looked up at her mother.

When Kayla finally confessed that she was going on a date with Richard, Margo was uncomfortable. There was no basis for the uneasiness except for the fact that Richard was white. "He ain't from our world, Kayla."

Margo had worked with white people for years, but that was work. She earnestly tried to repress her shadowy thoughts about their history, but they came flooding in anyway.

The days when black families on Caribbean islands sold their young daughters to white plantation owners for a small price just to make ends meet or to pay off a debt they had no choice but to be burdened with. Worried, but smart, parents would ship their girls to the island of Bermuda just to escape that fate. "I ain't selling you out to no white man. You hear me?" Margo looked at Kayla.

"You ain't selling me out, Mommy. I want to go on a date with him. This is my choice."

Margo had done everything in her power to ensure that her children's lives weren't a reflection of the horrid past of their ancestors. That was why she emphasized education and hard work. Over and over again, she battled with them to watch their company. Margo tightened her lips, exited her room and paced towards a window in the living room.

Kayla followed behind her mother.

Margo exhaled. Her gaze landed on the group of guys sitting on the crusty steps. She focused on the back of one particular head. Kayla imagined who had captured her mother's attention, but she kept her eyes fixed on her mother's tired face. She and her mother had been here before. The talks, the threats, the tears.

"We been through this already, Kayla."

"Mommy, it's not the same."

In all honesty, this Richard guy was nothing like Omari. At least Richard had a job. "I don't want you to miss out on someone special, but I don't want you to get hurt again either. You understand?" Margo was torn. She kept her gaze fixed outside. "Kayla, I hope you know what you doing. You need to be careful. Men don't give things unless they want something in return."

Her mother's counsel was stifling. Kayla exhaled. "I'll be careful, Mommy. I promise. And, please don't tell Mally anything just yet."

"I promise, but be careful," Margo warned.

Kayla kissed her mom and went into her room. She stood in front of her small closet that overflowed with clothes and shoes. "Hmmm...what to wear?" she said to herself and began her expedition.

A date, any date, let alone a first date was a distant memory for Kayla. Talking of dates, had she ever been on a real one like this? She remembered hanging out at house parties or limin' at festivities, but this was different. Kayla was never *asked* out on a date.

She just heard, "Jam this Friday. Leh we go."

With less than twenty-four hours to figure it out, she was uptight. Kayla didn't want to underdress for the date. Yet, overdressing would give Richard the impression that she was too eager. At last, she settled on a coral and blue, large print floral summer dress, with a jean jacket and a pair of beaded sandals. She would almost be ready for the date if it were not for the pins and needles.

CHAPTER 19

It was Friday. The anticipated date that was a few hours away could turn out to be a wonderful memory or an unforgettable disaster.

Richard was unusually edgy all day. He got a few "What's your problem" looks from Marisol's direction. His upcoming date with Kayla was throwing him off his game. He was hoping she would like the restaurant. He was hoping they would have a good time. He was hoping...well, no, he wasn't trying to impress her. If he were, he would be wasting his time; but he was hoping she would like him. "Just show her a good time," he kept saying to himself for the whole day. "Stay calm, Richard. Stay calm." His stomach suddenly felt hollow and vulnerable, yet full of anticipation.

Kayla's Friday was slowly creeping along. Looking at the clock was pointless. There was virtually no progress. In the morning her rounds were in slow motion, and in the afternoon the time in class stood still. Questions, comments, and participation that were usually on point, were non-existent.

"Kayla, is everything OK?" asked Nurse Analyn.

"Yes, I'm fine. Why?"

"You were very quiet today in class. Was everything clear?" Nurse Analyn asked.

"Yes, everything was clear."

"I just missed your comments, that's all." The instructor touched Kayla's shoulder and walked away.

The thought of going on a date with Richard had Kayla tied up in knots. It was overwhelming. She was going against her brother's advice; she was replaying her mother's warning, but she was still heading down the road. This was all so familiar. She was hoping tonight wouldn't be the beginning of the past. She was hoping it would be worth it.

At four-thirty in the afternoon, Richard finally wrapped up his day at the office. He was anxious to get home, shower, and dress. A pair of khaki pants was selected along with a dark blue short-sleeved shirt. As he buckled his belt and looked at himself in the mirror, he could see that his face was flushed; in fact, it was red all over. *This is crazy*, he thought. *Calm down, calm down, Richard.* The man who hadn't prayed in years, suddenly felt that this seemed like a good time to start again. He took a deep breath, looked at himself in the mirror again and said: "You got this!" He put on a pair of casual loafers and was out the door.

Kayla was glad that her mother had taken her kids to the park to give her some time alone to get dressed. She took her time to make sure that every element of her ensemble was carefully placed. She started with her naturally, coily mahogany-colored hair that was still reeling from the perfect twist out. She plaited a braid from one ear to the next to form a band in the front and she left the rest of her curls untamed in all their glory. She then slipped on her floral dress and a jean jacket. Kayla looked at her face in the mirror and applied a light foundation to her skin.

Next, she took her dark blue eyeliner and made a modest-sized line on her eyelids right above her eyelashes. Finally, Kayla colored her lips with subtle, matte red lipstick. She examined herself in the mirror. She was pleased.

It was six-thirty, time to leave the apartment to meet Richard at the gas station for seven o'clock. She wasn't quite sure that she wanted Richard back in the parking lot until she had explained a few things to him about her neighborhood. Would the guys on the steps intimidate him? He was totally oblivious to the dangers when he had dropped her home a few nights ago. *Imagine he wanted to walk me to my door. Who does that in Sofarelli?* Kayla crinkled her nose.

Kayla put on the beaded sandals that were waiting for her by the door and was on her way to start another chapter or at least turn another page in her life. She scurried down the stairwell, scooted past the guys on the step and cruised up the wide and very long road. The air was brisk but pleasant enough to calm her nerves and think about the evening that awaited her. What did Richard expect from her? What kind of women was he used to dating? Kayla wasn't sure, but she just wanted to be herself. Was she really his type or was he after something else as Mally had insisted?

Turning back did cross her mind a few times, but something told her to wait and see. Kayla hadn't been standing on the corner for very long when she saw Richard's truck in the distance. The glistening blue exterior heading toward her reminded Kayla of the day of her interview. The driver of a shiny blue truck held up traffic to allow a hen and her clutch of chicks cross the street. *Could that have been Richard?*

Richard arrived just in time to rescue Kayla from the ogling eyes of the guys who hung out religiously on the corner. She opened the passenger door and hopped in.

"Good evening, Richard."

"Hi, Kayla. How are you?"

The scent of juicy berries exploded in his cab.

He admired the sandals she wore with beads in colors that complemented her dress, and her toes were nicely polished in light pink.

She saw Richard glance over at her absorbing everything like he was making a mental note of what he was seeing. "I'm fine and you?" Kayla smiled at him. She felt herself blushing like a shy six-year-old.

"I'm doing fine." Richard smiled back at her.

Both lied.

They were totally winded trying to get ready for this evening. Fortunately, neither of them could tell what the other had endured from the moment this date was on.

For the first time, Richard saw her hair out in all of its splendor. He noticed the plaited cornrow braid forming a band in front that went from one ear to the other. He liked how the rest of her hair was out free to do its own thing at the back of her head. This was a woman who embraced her natural beauty, and it was radiating. Richard was charmed by the colorful floral dress which was topped off with a jean jacket. Understated. He liked that. And...ahhh...that lingering fruity fragrance that he couldn't really identify but liked very much.

Richard turned left at the gas station continuing westward into the heart of Frederiksted.

"So, where are we heading?" Kayla was clueless about what Richard had in mind. He had never answered her text when she had asked.

"Don't worry. 'Follow your nose,' my father used to say." Richard flew by the colorful buildings in town, and soon the outline of a dark red structure came into view. They were passing Fort Frederik.

Then, Kayla sighted the once popular, but now forgotten Paul E. Joseph Stadium across from the beach park that swarmed with people during Sunset Jazz. The road ahead darkened as street lights became fewer. "Hope you don't plan to kidnap me," she said and looked over at Richard.

He smiled. "Nah."

A house or two was seen as they moved deeper into the West. Eventually, he stopped at a place that looked like an old chattel house painted in bright blue and yellow. The lighted sign on the side of the road read "Sunny's Beach Bar and Grill".

"Here we are!" Richard announced.

Kayla sighed with relief and smiled. He hadn't kidnapped her, and she had dressed appropriately.

CHAPTER 20

Richard parked across the street from the restaurant in a clear spot large enough for his Raptor™. "Wait, Kayla. Let me get the door for you," he said and zipped around the back of the truck to the passenger side.

He opened the door and helped her out of the truck. For some reason, the last time he gave her a ride she'd made it seem as if it were too dangerous for him to come out of his truck, let alone, open the door as a proper gentleman should.

"Thank you," Kayla said as Richard held her hand to help her down.

They strolled side by side across the street toward the restaurant.

"I hope you like it."

"I'm sure I will."

Richard let Kayla enter first, and then he followed. The place was slightly run-down but cozy. There was reggae music jamming. The band was blowing up the place, killing it with their performance of "Rockaway" by Beres Hammond. Richard had made reservations just in case the place was full, and it was. The special table under the tree was theirs. It was on the deck instead of the sand and had an excellent view of the ocean. It was his favorite spot. There was an umbrella for shade from the sun or protection against anything, like an iguana, that might unexpectedly plop down on the table.

The couple was led to the spot reserved for them. Richard nodded to the regulars and spotted two familiar faces--Mark and Barbara Cohen

Richard pulled out a chair for Kayla, and she sat down. "That man over there in the pinstripe vest looks familiar," Kayla said.

"Who? Mark Cohen?" Richard asked as he pulled out a chair to sit.

"I don't know his name."

"He is a client."

"Oh, so you know him?"

"Yeh, I do. Where have you seen him before?"

"I don't remember, but his face is familiar."

"Anyway, enough about other people--," Richard said. "Would you like something to drink?" He changed the subject. It didn't matter too much to him the stares from strangers, but he didn't know what to make of the ones from the Cohens. Obviously, Kayla had noticed too.

"Cranberry juice is fine, thanks." Kayla cleared her throat wondering if she looked nervous, because she certainly felt it.

"OK. Wait here. I'll be right back." Richard moved away from their table and walked toward the dimly lit bar. He left his citrusy, wildflower fragrance lingering at the table.

Kayla watched Richard as he swaggered over to the bar. Put simply, he was fine. Her seat gave her a vantage point she had never enjoyed before.

A warm sensation overpowered her.

Richard approached the tall, middle-aged Rastafarian bartender. The Dread had his head wrapped in large ice (red), gold (yellow) and green turban with black accents. Judging by his age and the size of his turban, Richard suspected that his dreadlocks were past his waist, if not floor length.

The bar had its own understated vibe going on. Bunny Wailer roots reggae was coming through the large speakers that were strategically placed on either side of the counter. For anyone sitting at the bar counter, this reggae almost drowned out the reggae the band was playing across the way on stage. Multi-colored spotlights illuminated a few overlapping rusty corrugated galvanized sheets that created a rustic backdrop for long glass shelves that supported tons of liquor bottles of all shapes and sizes.

"Yeh de man. What can I do for you?" the Dread asked in a hoarse, thick voice.

"A cranberry juice and a club soda, please," Richard requested. His hands were in his pocket trying to control his nerves.

"Irie, man." The bartender said and prepared the glasses with ice and poured the appropriate liquid in each glass. He placed the two well-prepared drinks in front of Richard.

"Thanks," Richard nodded as he picked up the drinks and started to walk away.

"Hey, yo," the Rasta called out to Richard, "You know that you're dining with an empress, right? Make sure you treat her like royalty."

Seriously! Richard thought. He was desperately struggling to avoid the anxiety of trying to measure up to a standard someone dared to set for him. The pressure was on, and this was only the first date. He was expecting that an interracial relationship would arouse feelings in others, positive or negative. Who knew? Now, he understood the strange looks from both blacks and whites as he and Kayla stepped into the place. Richard nodded to the bartender and continued toward the table, drinks in hand.

Kayla saw the irritated look on Richard's face as he made it back with the drinks. He placed her drink in front of her and sat down. "What's wrong?" she asked as she took a sip from her glass. "What was the Rasta telling you at the bar?"

"Something about your being an empress and that I had better treat you like royalty," he muttered.

Why was Richard puzzled? She wondered. *Did he plan on mistreating me?* The Rasta was only looking out for her. Kayla felt that was cool. Again, Mally's words began their jingle in her ears. On the other hand, Kayla stopped to consider how pressured Richard might be feeling. He was white and dared to hang out with a local young lady who was not even in his social class. Yet, his reaction made her question whether his motivation was somewhat spiritual or purely carnal? It was becoming clear to her what they would be up against if they decided to pursue this relationship. "We can leave if you feel uncomfortable," Kayla suggested, testing to see if Richard's motives were sincere.

"No, of course not, I'm fine," Richard said. "We can't always run away every time someone comes to us with stuff we don't like. We would be reduced to meeting up only in private."

"You do know that even if we were the same race we would still have challenges. I've had some serious trials with black guys, and I'm sure you've had your share with white girls, too."

Richard looked over at the lovely woman dining with him. Her words made so much sense. A sharp feeling shot to his core. Not the warm tingling, blood rushing feeling. This time it was a feeling of pride. She was an empress!

That little chit chat impelled them both to make the best of the evening. In time, a short, stocky waitress with a thick Crucian accent came over to take their orders. She was elated to see one of her favorite customers. Apparently, Richard was more of a regular than he cared to admit.

"Richie, you back!" she said and winked at him.

"Yeh, you know I have to come see you, Clara," Richard said smiling.

"The usual?"

"Yep."

Clara jotted down Richard's selection. She knew it by heart-- grilled Mahi Mahi with seasoned rice, stewed beans and steamed vegetables.

"And you?" Clara looked over at Kayla.

"I'll have curried chicken, white rice and coleslaw. Thank you."

When the food arrived, it was clear that the chef had no plans on letting them down. The food was absolutely amazing.

Kayla said, "Do you know that some people say that nothing unites people more than eating together.' She winked and smiled at Richard.

"You sound like a poet or something," Richard said.

"I love quotes. They're gems of wisdom wrapped up into a few words."

He flashed a smile back at her and remembered his partner Clay, *She got brains.* Obviously, growing up in a government housing community had no bearing on her intellectual capacity. Would he have been less capable of becoming an engineer if he had grown up in that type of community? *The capacity would be there, but not the opportunity; it was just circumstance,* he thought. *That's all.* He was captivated by his date. She was definitely someone he wanted to get to know better.

"So do you have Crucian friends?" Kayla asked after the waitress cleared the table. Kayla hoped that Richard's answer would give her a hint into his motive for asking her out. Some white people came to the island and stuck to themselves, living as far away as possible from the locals. They mingled just enough to get whatever they wanted, and then they retreated into their private world--the no-go-zone they'd set up on an island full of black people. Others, in contrast, integrated with locals, embraced the culture, the food and even the dialect. Which group did Richard identify with?

"You mean Crucian or do you really want to say black?"

"Well, both," she said.

"Well, both," he answered.

"Ah right then, Mr. Patterson." She stirred the ice in her glass with the straw.

"So what about you? Do you have white friends?" He took a sip from his second glass of club soda.

Kayla had honestly never considered it the other way around. *Prejudice does go both ways,* she thought. Did she have white friends? "Would my boss, Mrs. Merchant, count?" she asked.

"No."

"Then, no."

"Interesting," Richard said, raising his brows.

"But that's not fair."

"Why not?" He stared at her.

Kayla looked up at the moon. "Well, I've always lived on St. Croix, surrounded by black and Hispanic people. White people hardly ever come around us. Or, let's just say I don't go where they are."

"Okay. You have a point," he said. "I'll ask you that question when you move to Iowa."

Kayla opened her eyes wide. "That will be the day," she said and the two cracked up laughing.

With no hint of trepidation, Richard asked Kayla, "So why don't you do that with your hair?" A black girl had just walked by with a very long, straight, shiny jet-black hair weave.

"What?!" Kayla couldn't believe Richard had gone there. Most black guys knew not to discuss a woman's hair except to compliment the style, color or length.

"Use a wig or whatever that is?" Richard pointed with his nose, a skill he had picked up from his island friends.

"That's a weave. And...? Why? You don't like my twists?" Kayla pursed her lips and tilted her head on one side.

"No, I love them," Richard confirmed. "It's just that I see a lot of black women doing that to their hair." He was still eyeing the girl as she sat down at a table to meet with her date.

"Well, there could be a few reasons why black women wear weaves," Kayla began, defending her sisters. "Some of us want to protect our natural hair and some of us think we have bad hair since everyone says so."

"Who is everyone?" interrupted Richard.

"White people," Kayla blurted.

"White people say your hair is bad?" Richard disapproved, doubting that her statement was completely true.

Well, in the past they did make us feel that our hair was bad," Kayla continued her debate standing tall on her imaginary soapbox. "What we saw on the cover of Vogue or Cosmopolitan, or whatever other magazine wasn't a black woman with natural hair. Any black person who wanted to move up in music or in the corporate world had to look more white than black. Even the men were straightening their hair. I'm sure you know that."

"I never really noticed," admitted Richard. Maybe Kayla had a point. This type of conversation was all new to him.

"Cause you're white, Richard," Kayla said as if their differences were a secret.

"I don't think white people mind your hair so much now. Maybe ...maybe black people make other black people feel bad about their hair, too. Have you ever thought about that?" Richard pointed out, almost certain he was laying bare other issues.

"'No hair is good or bad', my mother used to drill, '--only different textures.' Still, I used to be set on taking the every-six-weeks-relaxer jaunt to the hairdresser ever since I was thirteen."

"That must have been exhausting."

"Yeh. And there were tons of split ends and chops to cut off split ends, which were caused by the relaxer in the first place. Finally, a Halle Berry cut was the answer to my thin, lifeless hair that was once fast-growing and thick. Besides all of that, I had to endure scores of chemical burns on my scalp which turned into ugly scabs."

"Burns?"

"Yeh. And this was all done in an attempt to 'fix' my hair texture-- one that was just fine from the very beginning." She exhaled. "You know, it's true. We do have this 'good hair/bad hair' drama going on still. But...whatever. I love my natural hair."

"Well, I love your natural hair too." He leaned in closer to Kayla and realized that the insane juicy, berry fragrance was actually coming from her hair. "What do you have in your hair that's so delicious?"

"It's a gel infused with mixed berries and Argan oil," Kayla revealed, surprised he'd even noticed.

In reality, the fragrance was set in Richard's memory from the first day he met her. "I like it," he said.

As they came to the end of their dialogue about natural black hair, "She's Royal" by Tarrus Riley pierced through the air.

"Want to dance?" Richard asked, reaching for her.

Kayla looked at him in disbelief, doubting that he would do any justice to the song on the dance floor. She had seen a lot of white people try to dance Reggae or Soca or any other genre of music with a soulful beat. Basically, she didn't want him to embarrass himself nor was she prepared to be pitied on the dance floor. So far the evening was going well, and Kayla didn't want it to end on a sour note. She tried to decline, but Richard was insistent. Against her better judgment, she accepted warily.

They walked over to where a large group was already grooving to the pulsating beat. There were some funny stares, but the pair was undeterred. They had already committed to doing this thing. Richard held Kayla close with his hand around her waist, and he started moving. She followed obediently. Kayla could feel the rhythm coming through with every movement of Richard's body.

There were some raised brows on the dance floor. Heads cocked in astonishment.

Richard had surprised them.

He had surprised Kayla.

This dude is a boss on the dance floor, she thought. "Who taught you how to dance like this?" she whispered in his ear.

"You're not the only black person I know. Remember?" Richard said, and his body kept moving without missing a beat.

"OK, Mr. Patterson," she giggled.

If the dance was any indication of how this relationship might progress, Kayla would never want it to end.

Another song was blended in, but Richard took Kayla's hand and led her in the direction of the sandy beach a few feet away. The bluish tropical moonlight was gently caressing the waters of the majestic ocean. The waves were graciously rolling in to greet the shore with constancy. It was a commitment between the two that would never be broken. There were laughing gulls close by, cackling to each other, and very likely warning about the two visitors that were invading their territory. A gentle wind was blowing, lightly distributing the strong salt air.

As Richard steered Kayla closer to the ocean, the fine powdery sand found its way between her sandals as her feet became buried with every step. He looked down worriedly at her feet, and they both decided to continue their stroll barefoot. The water was warm and inviting. It was a comforting reminder of the blazing hot sun that stood in its customary position a few hours earlier.

"Creation is amazing," she said, taking a deep breath.

They meandered along the beach away from the crowd and the music. The conversation was about everything.

"So, how old are your kids?" Richard decided to ask.

"Seven and five. Do you have kids?" she asked.

"No," he said.

"Do you want kids?"

"Someday, sure. It's a lot of responsibility. How do you manage being a single mother?"

She smiled at the moon and inhaled. "Mothers do not get a day off. Every waking moment is centered on your kids. To be honest, I couldn't do it without my mother. As you can see, she is babysitting for me tonight."

"The pavilion...or the housing community."

"What about it?"

"Why was it so dangerous for me to walk you to your door?"

"Richard, have you ever been to the projects? Government housing communities can breathe a lot of undesirable situations."

"And you feel safe there?"

"Well, that's what we know. We learn to live with it. Everyone knows who belong there, and the guys know that you don't. I just wanted you to be safe."

"I see."

"Enough about me--What kind of work do you do? I know you're doing work at the hospital."

"I'm an engineer. So I'm not stalking you."

Kayla cracked up laughing. "And tell me about your friend."

"Friend?"

"You know who I mean."

"At Jump Up?

"Yes."

"Jennifer?"

"Why were you two together that night at Jump Up if she is only a friend, as you say?"

"It's a long story, Kayla. But, trust me, we are just friends." This interchange with Kayla wasn't like the battle Richard had fought with Jennifer the night at Jump Up; it was like a nice game of catch between two friends who wanted to see the other prevail.

At eleven-thirty Kayla said "I have to get home, Richard."

Richard cleared the bill, left a tip and went back to the Rasta at the bar. "You're right. She is an empress, bro. Thanks for looking out for her."

They bumped fists and Richard went for Kayla and escorted her out of the restaurant. He opened the passenger door for her and made sure she was in comfortably. He got into the driver's seat and they were off to the pavilion. He knew the drill. He understood it better now that she had explained to him a little more about the dangers of her neighborhood during their conversation on the beach.

When Kayla entered the apartment, all of the lights were off except the one in the hallway. She went into her kids' room to kiss each of them good night knowing that in a few hours the two would be making their nightly sojourn into her bed. She went into her mom's room to check on her too. While she was there she looked out the northern window. She saw the glow of the truck's tail lights, and her phone beeped.

"You OK?" Richard's text came through.

"Yes, I'm fine. I had a good time tonight. Text me when you get home," Kayla typed.

"I enjoyed myself tonight too. I'll text you when I get home," Richard promised.

That night Kayla lay in her bed sandwiched between her two kids and thought about the possibility of marrying Richard.

Planning the wedding would be crazy. He would decide to hire a wedding planner. Kayla wouldn't have the time between being a mother, working and studying. Apart from Kayla not having the time, he would know that he didn't have the strength to go through this without professional help. Kayla wanted a traditional religious ceremony in a building designed specifically for that purpose. It was Margo's dream for her daughter. She had never had that for herself. The least Kayla could do was to grant her mother that wish.

Then, of course, the colors would be chosen. Kayla wanted a berry-hued, wine-inspired jewel toned wedding. She wanted a three-tiered wedding cake decorated with berries and flowers. She wanted an evening reception. There was a long list of what she wanted.

Kayla stopped herself. Her mind was going too far. This was the type of "Omari" dreaming she kept trying to avoid.

CHAPTER 21

The next morning Richard picked up his phone and typed, "Good morning ☺," then he hit the send button.

"Hey, morning," Kayla replied.

"Everything OK?" Richard asked.

Kayla sensed genuine concern. "Yeh 👍, why?"

"Just want to make sure. How is your mom, Samaria and Adjoni?"

"Mom is fine, washing. Kids, sleeping ☺."

"My friend, Clay, is getting married in a few months. Would you like to come with me as my date?" Richard stared at his message and then waited. Was he really doing this? He pressed "send".

"The one I met at Jump Up?" typed Kayla.

"Yes," Richard confirmed.

"Are you sure they won't be expecting you to bring your *other* friend ☺?"

"I think we went over this already," Richard responded, shooting down that thought.

"I accept 😁," she smiled to herself. She was sure he felt it.

"RSVP 2," Richard typed and hit the send button to Clay's number.

It was Saturday. Richard had to pick up Jamal. Before his date with Kayla last night, Richard figured that Clay and Jamal understood each other and that's why they hit it off so well. Now, he was miffed. Was he even trying hard enough to get to know the young man? Jamal lived in a government-owned housing community like Kayla's.

Richard picked up Jamal from the Center in downtown Christiansted. Although Richard knew where Jamal lived at his grandmother's, he had never been there. The rules were clear: all the participants had to meet at the center for a motivational speech, after which they would mingle for a while and then everyone would leave. Drop off was at five o'clock, back at the center.

Today, Richard planned to bring Jamal to his home for the first time. He had to spend some time with Jamal for a while to see what kind of youth the young man was before inviting him to the house. That was due to a recommendation from a counselor at the center, as well as his better judgment and Clay's strong suggestion.

Richard had taken Jamal on hikes and walks through the rainforest and on the scenic route in Frederiksted. They took a trip to Buck Island on a snorkeling tour. They did a little league baseball game at Matthew Charles Park, or "Machuchal" as the Latin locals called it. They even went to a basketball game at Jamal's school.

Also, as per Clay's advice, Richard had planted a few dollars around his truck as a test. The youngster checked out. He was a good kid who happened to be living with bad circumstances. His sisters lived with their aunt in a different housing community. They were also part of the program.

Today, Richard wanted Jamal to help him with the renovating of one of the rooms in his house, which included installing sheetrock. He wasn't an expert, but he could teach Jamal whatever he knew. With a little more insight into Jamal's world through his new *friend*, Richard was hoping he would be able to concentrate enough to be an attentive and instructive mentor. But with all his good intentions, his mind was deep into Kayla. Everything about her was so intriguing.

Richard could picture Kayla in the room with them as they worked on screwing in the sheets and taping up the seams. He had filled her in on quite a bit about the renovation on their ride home from the hospital. He had told her so many things about the journey, and he sensed that she found his stories very entertaining. He wanted to invite her to see the house, to see his handiwork. She did tell him that she wouldn't mind coming by.

Miles away in Frederiksted, Kayla was trying to keep her mind off Richard. The date the night before was unexpectedly enjoyable. It's not that she didn't expect to enjoy the date, but it exceeded her expectations. *Richard and I are so different*, she thought. They were from distinct worlds; yet somehow they clicked. How was that possible?

In the middle of the usual housework commotion on Saturday, there was a knock at the door. Margo eyed Kayla as she headed to her room with clean bed sheets in hand. They were not expecting anyone, unless one of the neighbors wanted a cup of soap powder because they had run out. Saturday was the official wash day in the neighborhood. The hum of washing machines could be heard in almost every building.

Kayla opened the door.

A stout white man stood there. He wore a pinstripe suit without the vest, and his hair was pulled back in a ponytail. She remembered him from the restaurant the night before. Kayla wondered why his face was familiar. Obviously, she was missing something. How did he find her, and what did he want?

"So, how much do you charge?" he asked Kayla in a strong Brooklyn accent.

"Wha' you mean by dat?" Kayla asked in her distinct Crucian accent.

"Yeh, how much do you charge for your services?"

"Wha' services you talking about?"

"I saw you with a white guy last night. How much he paying you?"

"Paying me? I don't know wha' you talkin about." Kayla attempted to slam the door, but the man jammed the door with his foot.

"Look. I don't know what Richard wants with you, but he is already seeing someone else. I'm sure he told you."

Kayla glared at the man. Who was this fool harassing her, and why the visit? The conversation was making her nervous, but she was determined not to show any fear. He was on her turf. One scream and the guys downstairs would rush to her aid. She was sure of it. Although she did wonder how this white man had passed by them in the first place.

"I mean, honestly, why would a guy like Richard be interested in you? Who are you? What do you have?" The man peeked through the partially opened door into the apartment. "Obviously, nothing." He looked back at Kayla. "Look, I can double or triple whatever you get. You want $1,000? What about double that? I'm sure it will go a long way."

"I ain't want your dutty money." Kayla held the door tighter, ready to slam it and prepared to ignore any obstruction this time.

"OK. But leave Richard alone and stick to the guys who really want you," the man said and removed his foot from the doorway right before the steel door came into violent contact with the door jamb.

"Who was that by the door?" Margo asked, standing at the entrance of the hallway.

"Jehovah's Witnesses."

"And you slam the door, Kayla?" Margo had taught her kids to listen to anyone who came to talk to them about the Bible.

"I didn't mean it. It was the wind," Kayla said.

Margo looked at Kayla. "How was it last night?"

"It was OK."

Kayla went to the window and peeped through the louvers. She saw the man nod at the guys on the step and head over to a black Range Rover™ parked in the lot. She sucked her teeth and walked to her room. She needed some time to think about what had just happened. Telling her mother was out of the question. Her mother would freak out for sure. She would hunt the man down and find him. It would turn into a big thing. Kayla wasn't about to go through all that. But, there was something she was missing about this guy. She had recognized him last night. It turns out that he had recognized her too. But from where?

"Well, just be careful, Kayla," Margo said as she watched Kayla walk away. "Oh, I forgot to tell you," she continued, "the neighbors are having another block party tomorrow and I ain't missing it. You know food, drinks, bouncing castles, music--the works."

"Yeh. OK, Mommy," Kayla said, totally distracted by her thoughts.

"I'm taking Samaria and Adjoni. You can have the apartment to yourself to study. To catch up, you know."

"Okay. Thanks, Ma."

Kayla did plan to review her notes from Friday's class. That day she hadn't been able to concentrate at all. The thoughts of her date with Richard consumed her. But, today was shaping up to be worse. Her date with Richard had landed her an unexpected visit from a stranger who had a familiar face. Concentrating on her course was out of the question.

Before her visitor appeared, she was floating around the house with her head in the clouds. She was thinking about how Richard made her smile and laugh. That kind of attraction was strange to Kayla. The entanglement with Omari was like a fatal attraction, except for their kids. The other guys who tried weren't worth mentioning. She thought Richard was different. She had agreed to go out with a complete stranger; but look what had happened. Some fool came to pay her a visit, treating her like some kind of prostitute.

Her feet were back on solid ground now.

Maybe she should have declined to go out with Richard. Mally had warned her. Her mother told her to be careful. But there was something about Richard that seemed unusual, in a good way. There was something about the way he interacted with her that had caught her attention from the very beginning. He said he didn't have a *bodyguard*. He said she was only a friend. And he said he made that clear. But, suppose the man only wanted to scare her?

Well, it was working.

Her phone beeped. One message. It was Richard. "Can I see you tomorrow?"

Kayla blinked. She wasn't sure how to respond. If this was a regular day, she would have typed "OK" without hesitation. After her encounter with the man in the ponytail, however, nothing made sense. Was it too soon to see Richard again? Should she even see Richard again? She remembered the threat. They had a wonderful time last night, but this may be more than she had bargained for. Under normal circumstances she would have tried to take things slow, because it was so easy for things to spiral out of control. Frankly, things were already out of control. Despite that, she wanted to see Richard again. "How else can I get to the bottom of this mess if I don't see Richard again?" Kayla said to herself.

"Yes." She typed wondering if she should touch the "send" button on her phone.

Richard's phone beeped. One message. It was Kayla.

He was glad she agreed to see him again, but Richard couldn't help feeling a little nervous. He typed, "Is the afternoon around three o'clock OK?"

Kayla: "Yes"

Richard: "Can I pick you up from your apartment?"

Kayla: "Yes"

Richard spent the whole night cleaning and tidying up in preparation for his visitor. He was excited to show her what he had done with the place. Richard had already shown Kayla some 'before' pictures Friday night on the beach. Having her at the house to see the results would be special. He felt like a five year old anxiously waiting to show his parents his childish art project.

The next day, Richard showed up promptly at three o'clock in the afternoon. The drive from Kayla's apartment to his house would be a long one, and he was looking forward to the usual delightful conversation.

"So, how are things, Kayla?" Richard asked as he made a right turn at the gas station and headed down the long, seldom traveled road leading to the highway.

How are things? You tell me, she thought. This was the perfect time to ask him what in the world was going on. Why were strange men knocking on her door, threatening her? *What's up with that,* she wanted to ask him. "Okay," Kayla said.

"Why you so quiet? What's on your mind?"

Kayla wanted to scream. *Why was this turning out to be so confusing?* "Class," she said.

Richard looked over at Kayla with narrowed eyes. It was a straight shot from the west side to the middle of the island. The traffic light at the intersection of the Sunny Isle's Shopping Center presented some options, straight ahead towards Sion Farm or turn right and head towards the refinery. "So that's it--class?"

"Yes, and some other things."

"Like what? If you don't mind telling me."

"I mind."

"OK. I understand," Richard said, but he really didn't.

He veered to the right trying to avoid bumper to bumper traffic. He whirled southward in the direction of the refinery and then eastward to Christiansted town. He opted to drive through the scenic town instead of taking the bypass road. They approached the traffic light at Basin Triangle and turned right into the heart of Christiansted.

"So...,"

"Uh huh..."

"You said that you don't have a bodyguard, well--a girlfriend, a woman, a chick. Whatever you guys say."

"Yeh, that's what I said. Why?"

"It's just that..."

"Yeh." Richard tilted his head and maintained his easterly track out of the crowded town and onto East End Road.

"Forget it."

"OK. I'll forget it. Ever been to the East End?" Richard asked, glad to change the subject.

The East End Road led right past Cramer's Park Beach near Point Udall, the easternmost part of the United States of America.

"Yeh. For family picnics."

"Cramer's Park?"

"Yep. Of course, we never have the beach to ourselves, though. Tons of families would be there with the same goal in mind."

"And what's that?"

"Partying. My Uncle Zach would set up his stereo and six-foot speakers and the jamming would begin. Food and drinks can't done. Oh, sorry..."

"I understood you. You mean lots of food and drinks."

"Yeh, that's right." Kayla fixed her gaze on Richard. "So, anyway the kids would be in the water until they wrinkle. The feting would be from morning till night. Although, for some of my cousins the party continued into the next day, because they chose to camp out on the beach."

"Not going as far as Cramer's Park, though," Richard said and slowed down to allow a flock of unconcerned sheep cross the road.

They came near a narrow road with an illegible, weather-beaten sign that was most likely battered by a hurricane decades ago. Evidently, nobody had bothered to spare passersby the confusion by changing it or removing it. Naturally, the people who traveled the road regularly did not need a sign.

"On all my trips to East End I've never been to any of the houses we pass by, let alone the ones nestled in the hills."

"Well, I'm happy to give you your first tour." Richard navigated a steep driveway that cropped up. Kayla was shocked that Richard had lived so deep in the eastern end of the island. They swung past at least ten fairly large houses before pulling into his driveway.

Kayla looked at the scene. This was a high-end neighborhood, nothing like hers. She saw the garden he had been so animated about and recognized the Barbados Pride with bright orange flowers that was the star of the show. Beyond question, the house had exceptional curb appeal.

The night Richard had driven her home from the hospital he had described how hard it had been to get his garden growing. The persistent salt air and dry conditions in the East End were formidable forces. He spent most of his Friday evenings and weekends working on his house, he said. From what she could see, his hard work was paying off.

Richard opened the door, and Kayla was at a loss for words when she saw the interior space. The foyer was warm and classy, clad with mosaic slate and glass tiles on the ceiling and the walls on either side. It created a cocoon of light and dark gray hues with sparkles which danced as the beams of sunlight from the large glass windows grazed each tile. Directly in front was a spectacular view of the serene cosmic ocean and the far watery horizon. The kitchen was modern with sleek chestnut brown wood grain cabinets, white quartz countertops and black slate appliances. Kayla was impressed.

"This is beautiful, Richard," she said softly.

"Let me show you around to the back," he said, reaching for her hand and leading her down a very wide, long hallway.

He showed her the master bedroom he had recreated.

"Simple. I like it. The view is amazing!" she said.

They walked around in the rooms that were still under renovation as Richard explained what his plans were for each space. Suddenly, Richard's phone rang, interrupting the tour. It was his mom. He had to take the call.

"Excuse me," he whispered.

"Okay." Kayla excused herself so that Richard would have his privacy.

She went back into the living room to take in the view of the vast, wavy ocean again. There were miles and miles of beautiful dark blue water with no end in sight. Her mind wandered. Should she ask about the man with the ponytail? What was his connection to Richard other than just being a client? The long ride here had given her enough time to broach the subject, but she couldn't.

Richard hung up the phone, leaving his mom still ignorant of the fact that her son had a special visitor with him in his house. He saw Kayla standing by the large glass windows looking outside. Kayla's eyes were fixed on the view. She was definitely awestruck. It made her speechless, she had told him earlier. He was in awe as well, but of her.

Richard slowly moved towards where Kayla was standing.

Suddenly, the familiar warm sensation overtook him and the blood began rushing through his body taking its position. He wanted her. Badly. The feeling was strong, unbearable. He walked up behind her and put his hands on her shoulders.

Kayla felt Richard's warm breath caress her neck.

He kissed her on one side of her neck and then the other. The sweet scent of berries was driving him crazy.

Kayla felt the warm sensation too, and his cologne with perfectly blended notes of flowers and wood was adding fuel to the fire. She was ready to receive his love, all of it. There was no doubt about that either. But was it love? How could she be sure that this was the right time?

She felt like she was falling into nothingness. She closed her eyes. The look on Mally's face the night at Jump Up appeared in front of her. The man at her door had asked her "Why would a guy like Richard be interested in you?" *Yes, why would he be?* Her mind flashed back to this same emotional spot, but with Omari. How many times would they do this *thing*, this dance, before Richard got tired of the music and decided to move on? Kayla knew from ex-perience that this was going to lead down a road she wasn't pre-pared to travel. She couldn't do it.

Kayla turned around to look Richard in the eyes. "Richard," she said softly and contemplatively, trying to choose the right words, "What do you think I want from you?"

"Like what?

"Like money."

"Money?!"

"Yes, do you think I'm trying to get money from you?"

"What?! I'm not sure where this is going."

"Look, Richard, there's a lot I don't understand--about you, about myself."

"Is this what you were thinking about on the ride here?"

"Yeh, that and other things. Anyway...look, I let my heart and feelings choose for me before, and it didn't turn out well for me."

Richard stared at her and said nothing.

Kayla continued. "I made a promise to myself that I would not go down this road again with another guy until I was sure, until I was positive, that he really loved me. A guy would show me that he really loves me by marrying me."

Yes, she said it. That's what she really wanted from a relationship--marriage. Was there something wrong with expecting commitment? How else would she know if a guy really loved her? Richard couldn't possibly love her. He hardly even knew who she was. After all, they had only been on one date.

Richard looked away and stared out into the distance for a few seconds. Then their eyes locked again. What Kayla saw in Richard's eyes was not what she had expected. She saw disappointment. She expected that. But she also saw reluctance, unwillingness. Her brother was right. Everybody was right--her mother and the man in the ponytail too. These guys didn't mind getting down, but they don't plan to stick around.

"You ain't gon be the girl on their arms in public places," her brother had warned her. Kayla was disappointed too. Disappointed in Richard, but even more in herself. She should have known better. How could she be so naive? They wanted different things.

"I guess I know where you stand, Kayla."

"Yes. It's how I feel. End of story."

"And I guess you're ready to leave now?" Richard asked.

"Yes," Kayla said softly.

The ride back into town was long and quiet. They didn't say much to each other. There wasn't much to say. A lot to think about, though. Kayla marveled at how taking sex out the picture can cause some relationships to fizzle out. It's as if hooking up was the only thing two people could ever have in common.

She was done. Done with the players, the games, the emotional roller coaster rides. Done. She wanted more for herself. Yes, sex was one way to express love or attraction, but it was not how to prove love. Kayla wanted someone to prove their love for her by being caring, loyal, honest and trustworthy. Richard had to prove his love for her before she went any further, and he was clearly not ready for that. Just as she had suspected, they were going very fast, heading nowhere.

Once they were out of East End and back into Christiansted town, Kayla asked Richard to drop her off on the side of the road. "I'll take a bus home," she said.

It would be a long bus ride from the heart of Christiansted to where she lived in Frederiksted, but she needed time alone, away from him. She had to think this through.

"I don't feel right dropping you off on the side of the road, Kayla. I picked you up from your home, and I want to take you back safe and sound."

"It's OK, Richard."

"Like some call girl. But, apparently that's what you think I have in mind."

"Just drop me off at the gas station by the Pueblo Supermarket."

"It's starting to drizzle, Kayla."

"I said drop me off. I don't care if it rains," Kayla said, blinking back the tears.

Richard sensed that he had offended her and had no choice but to respect her wishes.

He put Kayla off at the gas station on the corner. As he drove away, he stared into his rear-view mirror. The young lady who had charmed him from the moment he saw her was standing there in the rain looking so vulnerable. And he was to blame. A funny feeling came up in his heart. It was the pain of disappointment. He was disappointed in himself.

On the bus ride home, Kayla put her head against the window and stared outside. She saw buildings and cars and people and trees, lots of trees, everything moving by too quickly to focus on any one thing. A man invites a girl to his home--it wouldn't be to chit chat. What was she thinking? She was foolish to think that Richard was a different kind of man from Omari.

She had envisioned an exquisite venue. Clay would stand next to Richard as his best man. The ceremony would commence, the procession would begin with her two children, and then the bridesmaids would follow closely behind. Margo would appear at the entrance. Mally would enter with Kayla on his arm. All eyes would be on Kayla. What Richard had imagined had not come close to the reality. She was breathtakingly beautiful. Her gown would be a perfect blend of elegance and sparkle with a figure-flattering fitted bodice and sweetheart neckline. Her hair would be styled in an updo adorned with carefully placed diamond studs. Her face radiant with happiness. Their day had finally come. She needed to stop dreaming.

Curtains were up again, and Kayla was center stage. There were new actors now, different scenery, more props and, and as usual, a whole lot of drama. Just when Kayla thought she knew the plot, Richard had suddenly become the antagonist. At this point, Kayla could only think about the ironies playing out in her life.

CHAPTER 22

The next day, Richard was still checking his phone for messages. He had to have checked a million times. Was Kayla going to text... something ...anything? This fearless, self-assured man who had the guts to move thousands of miles away from the U.S. mainland to live on a little tiny island, take over an engineering company and ride out terrifying hurricanes, could not even muster up the courage to text a young lady to see if she had arrived home safely.

He officially declared himself a wimp.

Richard wondered what she thought of him now. Was there any way that he could make up for yesterday? He had moved too fast, even for himself. He'd spooked her. Clay had warned him, but he hadn't listened. He could only imagine what Clay would tell him if he found out. How could he fix this? "Just text something," he told himself. What's the worst that can happen?

"Hey," Richard typed.

Send.

Kayla's phone beeped. One message. It was Richard. *Really?* She thought.

She was in the middle of making her rounds. Kayla had a long day ahead of her, and she didn't want to deal with this right now. What would she say anyway? Kayla had lost her focus just like she had done in the past, but she was determined to get it back. Her relationship with Omari almost cost her a high school diploma. Now, she was finally making something of her life. Her dream of becoming a nurse was on the horizon. She kept telling herself that she had to stay focused.

Richard checked his phone.

No messages.

That night in class Kayla managed to pay attention. There was so much to learn. After class, Nurse Analyn approached her and said, "Kayla, you're back!"

Hopefully for good this time, Kayla wanted to say out loud, but she half-smiled instead.

Every day that passed by Kayla was sure that she would feel better. Richard had not been in her life before, and he would not be in her life again. She tried to convince herself that moving on wouldn't be that difficult.

Every day that went by intensified the battle between her heart and mind, and there was no umpire. She had fallen hard for this man and wanted to be with him. *Dreaming all kind of crap.* She scolded herself. But now she understood that for Richard this was not about commitment. He was a player, same as all of the others.

What had she missed? He hadn't seemed like that at first. Kayla looked at the text message Richard had sent her three days ago. What did he expect her to say? She knew that nothing she wanted to say would make sense to him. She still could not reply.

Richard checked his phone every day. There were tons of messages. Messages about work and one from his niece who sent him a photo of her new puppy. Nothing from Kayla. At this point, he was wondering if he needed to talk with Clay. He would have to humble himself and endure the well-deserved tongue lashing.

After two weeks had passed, Richard had to stand up--to himself.

"You busy? We got to talk," Richard typed, then pressed *send* to Clay's number.

"What's up?" asked Clay.

"Face to face," said Richard.

"Will be there in ten," Clay replied.

Clay got there in under ten minutes. It was obvious that his boss had something serious he wanted to discuss with him. Was there a problem with one of the projects? Did a client call complaining? He couldn't imagine what it might be.

Clay whisked passed Marisol whose back was turned to him, and he appeared in Richard's office.

"Close the door," Richard told Clay.

"This must be serious," Clay said. He closed the door and stood in front of Richard's desk. They usually discussed everything with the door opened. Even Marisol was privy to all the issues surrounding the projects.

Richard looked at Clay and cleared his throat. He was preparing himself for the whipping he was about to receive. Although it was hard for him to admit it, he needed Clay's advice.

"Look Clay," Richard began. "I know you told me about Kayla, about her being on lockdown and everything."

"Yeh."

"Well...we went out on Friday and had a really nice time."

"Uh huh."

"I think you need to sit down," Richard said, knowing that this "talk" was going to take a little longer than Clay had anticipated. It had nothing to do with work.

"So this is about Paradise Mart?"

"Yes, that is what I was saying. So, you see, we went out on Friday. Nice time and everything."

And...," Clay said waiting for more.

"But then there was a situation at my house the Sunday after," continued Richard.

"Your house?! She was at your house?!" Clay sat up.

"Yes, I kinda invited her to see the renovations I've made and stuff." Richard continued, "Then I kinda made a move on her and ..."

"You made a move? Like 'I want to sleep with you' kinda move?" Clay hollered, jumping out of his seat.

"Yes, that kind of move, Clay," Richard barked, getting frustrated.

"Slow your roll, bro," Clay told Richard. "This is all your fault."

"Yes, I know."

"So let me get this straight." Clay started enumerating. "You invite her on a date, she says 'yes'. You invite her to your house two days later, bad move by the way, but she says 'yes' anyway.

You're not satisfied with the baby steps you're making, so you try to make a move on her. Am I right?"

"Yes," Richard grunted, covering his face with his hands. He knew that Clay must think he was a fool. A guy gets a chance to go out with a girl, a nice girl, and then he moves too fast. Idiotic.

"Richard, this is basic Dating 101 stuff. I guess you didn't take the class," riled Clay, his hands rubbing his head.

Richard deserved everything his friend was throwing at him, but there was more. "So now she's not answering my text messages," Richard kept going, "because..."

"Because she thinks you're a player," yelled Clay. "I tried to warn you, man."

"I know, I know," Richard lamented.

"So what you going to do now?" Clay asked, staring at his boss.

"I have no idea." Richard walked over to the window and started watching people and cars go by. He knew that Clay wanted to lambaste him and tell him what an idiot he was for messing up such a perfect opportunity. Fortunately, he had a friend with a heart. Richard was sure that Clay could see that he was already hurting, so he was thankful to have his friend join him at the window.

Richard's phone buzzed. It was Mark Cohen. Richard had been expecting the call.

"Hey, Rich did you get the signed documents?" The burly voice came through the phone.

"Yes, thanks, Mark. We got them, and we'll start working on the changes straight away."

"Hey, Rich," Mark continued. "We're heading out west to Sunset Jazz this Friday. We have a few new interns and another junior lawyer who came onboard. Trying to show them a good time, you know."

"I'm not sure if I can make it. I have a lot on my plate, Mark," Richard said intent on not allowing *Banks and Cohen* to steal yet another precious Friday night.

"Jason and I were hoping to talk with you about another project we had in mind," Mark said, pressuring Richard.

Why does this feel like a set-up? Richard reflected. "OK, I'll see if I can come by."

"See if Clay wants to meet us there too," Mark added.

"No prob," Richard said, placing his thumb on the "hang up" button ready to press.

"Jennifer would like to see you there too," were Mark Cohen's last words.

Jennifer was the downright last person Richard wanted to see. "Sounds good, Mark," he said and hung up.

Kayla was making every effort to stay on the top of her game at work and in class. Pedro and Shameka were desperately on the lookout for any indication that she was seeing someone but Kayla was maintaining her silence.

"So how was your weekend Kayla?" Shameka asked her one day, searching for any trace of a significant other.

"A lot of housework," Kayla said without looking up.

"Housework all weekend? Girl, you need a life," Pedro chimed in.

If they only knew how much of a life she was having. Kayla was certain that the two of them would love all the gory details.

In the middle of the conversation, Kayla finished cleaning up her cart, parked it away, picked up her books, said 'goodbye' and headed to the meeting room. She would be the only one in the room for a while. It was only twelve thirty. If only she could concentrate, it would be an accomplishment. "Focus Kayla," she kept saying to herself. She took a textbook out of her bag and began reading. None of the words made sense.

Kayla stumbled home, physically, mentally, and emotionally exhausted. Unfortunately, kids are usually not good exhaustion detectors. No matter how tired she was, they still expected their fun-loving, upbeat mother to show up. With that being the case, she began her usual evening routine. The sequence was: the homework, the bath that no one wanted to take, the cartoon shows and the bedtime resistance song and dance. Kayla's body was moving, but her brain was slowly shutting down.

Her phone beeped. One message. It was Mally.

"Hey, Kayla. What's up, sis? Need a favor. Can you go to Sunset Jazz this Friday? My boys are performing again. I need you to record them and send it to me."

"OK," She typed back without even thinking.

CHAPTER 23

I t was Friday night and checking his phone for messages from Kayla was turning out to be a total waste of time. Richard was fairly certain that she really didn't want to speak to him or even see him again. He had made a dumb move, point blank; yet he wasn't completely convinced that he should give up at this point. The problem was that he honestly didn't know what else to do.

Richard was getting ready to meet the *Banks and Cohen* team which usually required some mental preparation, but knowing that Jennifer would be there made it worse. He couldn't deal with the pushiness, mainly from Mark. It just wasn't cool. He chose a pair of light blue jeans out of his closet, and he pulled on a gray, long-sleeved sweater. Once his socks were on his feet, he selected a pair of white sneakers, picked up his keys and his phone and headed out the door.

The *Banks and Cohen* clan seized a large section of the park with lawn chairs, blankets, and bodies who chose to stand around. There she was standing next to her father. Richard ran his hand through his hair. He couldn't believe that Jennifer was back in St. Croix for the summer interning at her father's law firm. At least Mark had given him a heads up. Clay was around somewhere. It was very rare that Richard made it to any function before Clay did.

Clay had already sent Richard a text: "We here and so is your girl Jen 😊. Where u?"

"We need some more drinks here," Mark said, always in control of every situation. "Jen, why don't you get a few more bottles of local drinks?

"You coming, Richard..." she looked over and said, "...to give me a hand?"

"Huh... Well... OK," Richard said in the middle of his conversation with one of the new interns.

The vendor was only a few feet away. What could Jennifer possibly say or do in that short space of time that would make him feel awkward? Once the task was over, he would avoid her like the plague and call it a night.

Clay and Adrianna decided to hang out for a while with the *Banks and Cohen* bunch and came over. Hanging out with a bunch of strangers wasn't their plan for the evening. The two were dying to walk and dance on the sandy beach alone.

As the day wound down, Kayla regretted agreeing to videotape the band at Sunset Jazz for Mally. Her brother usually got a willing and happy little sister to do things, but she hadn't considered the nonsense that was bugging her right now. After a long, tiring week of work and study she didn't feel in any mood to go out 'liming' or mixing with a large crowd. Not to mention how the incessant flashbacks of the impasse with Richard made every task twice as hard. Unfortunately, she didn't even have a friend she could call who would do the honors for her. Of course, her kids wanted to come, and she planned to drag her mother along as well.

Kayla's preparations to leave the house with her kids were not simple. "How can two little bodies have so many demands?" she asked herself. If one didn't like their pants, the other didn't want to wear the shirt selected. For Samaria, her hair was always an issue. Somewhere in her mind Samaria thought that she was a fashionista who always had a statement to make.

Naturally, Kayla wouldn't admit that her daughter got her fashion sense from her mother. She just worked around Samaria's wishes. Her kids were slowly draining what little energy she had managed to regenerate. Kayla chose to wear some distressed jeans, with a colorful bright pink, orange and white tunic, and some comfortable black strappy flats. The plan was to go to Sunset Jazz, wait for the band's turn to play, take the ridiculous video and come back home.

Margo finally found parking on King Street. There were tons of people milling around, much to Kayla's chagrin. Sunset Jazz was a great spot to chill out on the beach, listen to good music and enjoy good times with friends. Everyone brought their own chairs or blankets to sit on. It was meant to be relaxing. Kayla was going to try to enjoy the moment. Hopefully, tonight she could put Richard in the back of her mind. It would be worth a try. As usual, Samaria and Adjoni wanted to play in the kids' park across the street, so Kayla and Margo entertained them for a while. The adults eventually pried the kids away from the attractions and decided to move closer to where the action was.

Both Kayla and her mother each held on tight to collapsible chairs thrown over their shoulders with one hand, while gripping a child's hand with their remaining one. Yet, it was the children who were huffing and puffing after testing out every attraction in the park. As one would expect, they were now very thirsty and desperately wanted something to drink. The group headed towards a vendor cart to buy drinks before anyone died of thirst.

Kayla was drained. She would have given anything to be in her bed. People were crawling all over like ants, and vendors were swamped. *Lines, more standing,* Kayla thought and frowned. Her eyes were on Packo's vendor cart with the bright red umbrella. She had bought drinks from this cart before at the Agriculture Fair. She already knew her choice--Passion Fruit.

Richard and Jennifer left the group and walked toward the vendor cart. A few feet away from arriving at their destination, Richard noticed a group heading to the same vendor in their sightline. An older lady, a younger, and two kids. He immediately recognized the younger figure. It was Kayla. He wanted to turn back, jump in the ocean, and do something--anything.

Kayla stood in line and gazed around, marveling at how many people were at Sunset Jazz. Ambling forward, heading to Packo's cart was a couple. Something about the guy's gait seemed familiar to Kayla. *Richard!* She growled under her breath. He was with Jennifer.

That dog! Really!

The man with the ponytail was right. Richard was already seeing someone. Obviously, she wasn't "just a friend" as he kept saying. Kayla clenched her jaw.

Margo looked at her daughter. "Wha wrong?" she asked.

"Nothing, Mommy."

Richard and Jennifer descended on the unsuspecting vendor with the bright red umbrella while Kayla and her family stood in line. Richard froze. There was a stillness in the air. The kind of calm that takes place when the trade winds weaken and heavy rainfall is expected. *I should have stayed home tonight to work on my house,* he thought. Jennifer was standing next to him and Kayla was standing right in front of him. What were the chances? He wanted to hide his head in the sand.

It's Jennifer all right, Kayla thought.

She kept her eyes fixed on the list of drinks the vendor had hanging on a pole, but she couldn't read anything.

Margo started piecing two and two together. She could tell what was happening. She wasn't certain who the guy was, but she knew her daughter very well. Kayla was livid. This must be the "Richard" she had recently dated. "What you want to drink, Kayla? Margo asked her daughter.

"Choose anything, Mommy."

"Good evening," Richard said, greeting the older lady. *This must be Kayla's mother,* he thought.

Margo half-smiled with raised brows that said everything.

Then he greeted Samaria and Adjoni, "Hi."

They both raised their cute little hands to wave without uttering a word.

He said nothing to Kayla. The words would not come out.

Kayla bit her lip.

Clay was with the *Banks and Cohen* group looking on. He could see that there was no exchange between Richard and Kayla, yet they were standing right next to each other. This was the first project he could not handle.

Margo took the lead in getting the drinks for her grandchildren. She could tell that Kayla was in no state to handle anything right now.

Richard glanced over at Kayla. She was flawless, beautiful. He liked her a lot, and he was so sorry that he had hurt her. He saw the anger and disappointment in her face. He wanted to tell her, "This is not at all how it looks, Kayla." And he also wanted to say, "Jennifer means nothing to me." There was a whole lot he wanted to say, but he couldn't. Not here, not now.

Kayla, on the other hand, tried hard to avoid looking at Richard. Why should she? She would just see a blank face anyway. Everything was a blur. She couldn't even breathe. Imagine what her mother was thinking! "You see wha' a tell you, Kayla," she could just hear it. "Mally was right," her mother would continue.

Kayla's brother's words were ringing in her ears. "This is who Richard would be parading around with in public," she could hear him say. Kayla prayed for the ground to open up so that she could push Richard in. She was ready to leave, but then, she heard the name of the band being announced. They were about to perform. She touched her mother's arm, took her kids, and walked away. She decided to fulfill her promise to her brother as quickly as possible and then leave.

Clay rushed over to offer moral support, even if it was just to stand there next to his boy, Richard.

Kayla held up well enough to stumble into the apartment and head straight for the bathroom. She curled up like a baby and cried uncontrollably on the damp floor. She felt a nagging pain deep down inside. "Mally was right, Mally was right," she sobbed. She let the shower run so that the kids wouldn't hear her blubbering. Thankfully, nothing had happened at his house. She comforted herself with that one fact. The thing is, something had already developed in her heart. How quickly he had moved on. She hated him for that. The nerve of Richard to be dating Jennifer and still claim that they were only friends. He was a player, and Kayla was just a pawn in his game. He tripped her up, big time; and she had to pull herself together.

Margo knocked on the bathroom door when she felt that Kayla had enough time to grieve. She reminded Kayla of one of the quotes that she wrote in a scrapbook when she was in elementary school. "Don't jump to conclusions when you don't have all the information, Kayla," she said.

"Whatever!" Kayla wanted to scream. Leave it to her mother to add another dimension to any situation. "It's just that I keep making bad decisions, Mommy," she said, sobbing.

"But you don't know, Kayla. You see two people walking together and you assume things."

"That was the same woman who was with him at Jump Up."

"You ask him about her?"

"Yeh, he said they were just friends. Why would I go out with a man who already had a woman?"

"Don't jump to conclusions, Kayla. When wind blow, you see fowl bottom. The truth will come to light one day."

"Well, the wind blow real hard tonight." Kayla sobbed.

"We'll see, child. We'll see," Margo said and gently wiped away her daughter's tears.

The scene at Sunset Jazz tormented Richard all night. He could not sleep. He stood in the same spot where he had held Kayla that Sunday when she had come to the house. He ran his hands through his hair. Those stupid berries were upsetting his life. Richard stared into the distance. The view from the window revealed the vast expanse glowing in the brilliant, peaceful moonlight. There was a calmness about the ocean that captivated him. He squinted his eyes shut. *Why is my life just the opposite?* He had really messed up, and he had to fix this.

CHAPTER 24

Friday night was a disaster, Saturday was a blur, and Sunday didn't show much promise either. A little after midnight, a sharp stomach ache rattled Kayla out of her sleep. She felt seriously ill. She barely made it into her mother's room in search of help. Soon after, everyone was unceremoniously packed into the Honda and they pelted to the hospital emergency room. There were forms that Margo had to fill out asking for information about Kayla that her brain could hardly recall, height and weight. How was she supposed to know those things about her twenty-four-year-old daughter? Meanwhile, fortunately, both Adjoni and Samaria managed to stay asleep on the hard, uncomfortable, not to mention cracked up dark green bucket chairs in the waiting room.

When Kayla finally got attention, the ER nurse asked, "Can you remember anything out of the ordinary that you ate?"

Kayla was still disoriented. She had broken out in a cold sweat, was vomiting off and on, and her body was now too dehydrated for any more diarrhea episodes. "Well, I had some fungi and boiled fish," Kayla managed to disclose as she groaned in pain.

"Did anyone else in your family eat the fish?" The nurse queried as she watched the young lady deal with the excruciating pain.

"No one else wanted Cavalli," heaved Kayla.

"It looks like Ciguatera poisoning," the nurse said.

"Huh?" Kayla's brain was foggy.

"Fish poisoning," the nurse said. "We'll hook you up to some IV fluid and let you rest for a while. You will be fine in a few hours once the poison leaves your body."

The dreaded day had arrived. The one that Kayla knew would eventually be her fate. She had her first bout of fish poisoning from Cavalli. She loved eating fish, all kinds of fish; especially Cavalli and the fish head was her favorite part. She knew there was always a possibility of fish poisoning. *But isn't that the case with all fish,* Kayla convinced herself. Her Uncle Zach had brought a styrofoam container with stewed fish to the house. He knew his niece was a fish lover like himself. The fish was heavily sautéd with tomatoes, garlic and onions together with cornmeal fungi mixed with chopped okra. It was too hard to pass up. Kayla was willing to take her chances. This pain was crazy, though. And Kayla didn't know if she would ever want to smell fish again, much less eat it.

The emergency room stay lasted for about three hours. Once Kayla's condition was stabilized she was discharged and given a list of foods that she could eat--crackers, applesauce, bananas, to name a few. Thank goodness the kids slept through the ordeal, she thought, and were still sleeping when they arrived back home.

Margo had managed to prop them both up long enough to maneuver her way to the second floor of their building and into their beds again. To set out for work in a few hours, however, was out of the question.

Margo woke up at five-thirty, at the same time she always did every morning, so she hardly got any sleep. Her daughter was wiped out from the nightmare that had played out a few hours earlier. Margo had no choice but to begin preparing her grandchildren's bags for school. At six-thirty she would wake them up to help them get ready for school, and then to catch the bus. Margo decided that it would be best for her to stay home with Kayla, just in case. Her work was too far away to get back in the event anything went wrong. Besides, Kayla had been through a lot emotionally. That coupled with the fish poisoning worried Margo. She would call her job to let them know she wouldn't be in today, and she would call Mrs. Merchant to explain that Kayla was sick with fish poisoning.

Kayla slept for most of the morning. At about noon she crawled out of bed, but was still very weak from the pain that had crippled her earlier. Richard drama and fish poisoning, all in one weekend. It was unbelievable.

"How you feeling, Kay Kay?" Margo asked.

"Much better, Mommy," Kayla mumbled as she stood in front of the bathroom mirror. She was feeling much recovered from the fish poisoning. How she was feeling about Richard was another story.

Kayla finally showered, re-tied the scarf on her head, and went into the kitchen to start the process of putting food back into her stomach. For the moment, her diet was strictly crackers, bread, applesauce, and bananas. She sat on the couch with some applesauce and a banana; then began watching SpongeBob™ episodes on television.

✶✶✶

Richard had to speak with Kayla face to face to explain the mix-up she'd seen on Friday at Sunset Jazz. He could only imagine what she'd thought when she'd spotted him with Jennifer that night. His plan was to visit her during her thirty-minute lunch break.

Richard screeched into the hospital parking lot at exactly twelve fifteen. Clay heard the penetrating moan of the truck engine and looked over. He wondered why his boss was at the building site, because Richard only visited the sites at specific intervals or when there was a problem. But then Clay realized that Richard wasn't there to check on the project at all. In fact, Clay saw him moving away from his truck and towards the hospital entrance.

"He's going to right his wrong." Clay smiled to himself. "You handle your business, Boss."

Richard pushed open the cafeteria doors. This was only his second time in the place, and he didn't know what to expect. He stood close to the doors and looked around. It was lunch time. All the tables were full of diners. His gaze first went to the serving station where she had appeared from with the menu, the first time he came into the cafeteria. Then, he eyed the drink station where they had their first conversation.

There was no sign of Kayla.

He knew that her lunch break should be about this time. He carefully scanned the area again; still no sign of her. Richard was trying to avoid having to inquire, but he decided it might be okay to approach the young man behind the counter. For some reason, the female worker looked like she was quite capable of giving him a hard time.

Richard came near to the serving station. "Hi, I'm looking for Kayla. Is she in today?"

"Who needs to know?" the guy returned with a challenge.

"Umm...a friend," shot back Richard, which in retrospect he thought may not have helped the situation.

"I'm not at liberty to say," said the young man.

Pedro remembered Richard. This was the man Kayla had a conversation with at the drink station her first day on the job. The day he reminded her that she was here to work and not to consort with the diners. *So this is the person that Kayla is wrapped up with,* Pedro thought. *¡Que fuerte!*

Richard realized that he was getting nowhere using this approach. "Thanks for your help," he said and left. He sprinted to his truck and called Marisol.

"Hey, Marisol. I need you to do me a favor--personal."

"What's that, Boss?"

"Call the hospital, ask for the cafeteria, and then speak in Spanish looking for someone named Kayla. Pretend to be her friend."

"OK."

"Call me back when you get some information."

"No prob, Boss."

Richard knew Marisol would follow his clear instructions to a tee.

The phone rang.

"J. F. Luis Hospital cafeteria," the person answered.

"Hola. Mi nombre es Marisol, me gustaria hablar con... " Marisol started.

When Marisol got the information she needed, she called her boss. The task was complete. Kayla was home sick with fish poisoning.

"What do you give a person suffering from fish poisoning, Marisol?" Richard asked.

"Let me google it. I'll text it to you." Marisol was on the case like a champ.

Richard waited by his truck for the message to come through. He heard a beep. One message. It was from Marisol.

"My girl, Marisol," Richard muffled.

He read the message:

"Try bland foods, such as crackers, toast, and bananas. Avoid spicy foods, fried foods, dairy, and foods that are high in fat and sugar. Drink plenty of fluids, but avoid milk or caffeinated beverages, sports drinks, with brand names such as Gatorade, etc. These are not meant to be used to treat diarrhea."

"Thank you, Marisol. Good job!" Richard typed then pressed "send".

"No prob, Boss," Marisol replied.

With two shopping bags full of all of the things Google™ recommended, Richard headed westward toward Kayla's apartment. He selected iTunes and his Beres Hammond album started streaming via Bluetooth™. "Love From a Distance" began to permeate the airspace in his Raptor.

He was going to get this girl.

CHAPTER 25

At two o'clock in the afternoon, Margo was on the porch hanging out some sheets when she saw a streak of blue glowing through the corner of her eyes. She looked through the fashion blocks and spotted a flashy blue truck parked in the lot close to the building. A white man jumped out, gathered up two full bags of groceries into his arms and headed for the steps. He said something to the guys, and they moved out of the way to make a path for him to walk. Margo's hands flew over her mouth. "My word..." she muttered and laughed to herself.

She came inside and looked at the back of her daughter's head. Kayla was on the couch watching SpongeBob on TV. The girl had no idea what was about to happen. There was a knock on the door. Margo took a deep breath and opened.

"Hi. Good afternoon. I'm Richard."

"I know exactly who you are, young man." Margo said and smiled. "Please come in."

Margo shook her head and chuckled.

When Kayla heard the deep familiar voice, she jumped up off of the couch and stared in disbelief at the figure standing in the door-way. "Richard! Wha you doing...? How did you even get up here?"

"I just told them I was your boss. I guess I look like a 'Boss', so they believed me." He smiled warily hoping the joke would soften her.

Kayla wanted to burst out laughing, but she refused herself the luxury. Instead, she pulled herself up as erect as she was able and cut her eyes at him. Then, she pursed her lips and flounced to her room. She would hide out there until he was gone. For all she cared, he could spend the rest of the afternoon talking with her mother! She didn't want to hear anything he had to say.

Eventually, she heard a knock on her bedroom door. Her mother strolled in with her arms loosely folded.

Margo smiled. She could understand her daughter's pain. Heaven knows, she had endured her fair share over the years as well.

"Kayla," Margo began as she studied her daughter's teary eyes, "that young man traveled a long way to get here...and I don't just mean on the road in his shiny blue truck. I mean in his mind and in his heart. Give him credit for that. The least you could do is hear him out. Now, you go out there and listen to what the man has to say."

Listening to her mother had never resulted in any harm to her. Yet, Kayla couldn't help wondering if her mom felt sorrier for Richard than for her own daughter.

Margo left Kayla's room and went into her own bedroom to give the two some privacy. Kayla brushed back into the living area. Richard was there sitting motionless, staring down at the small dining table. The finger marks were still showing in his sandy colored hair where he had run his hand through over and over again. His light blue, short-sleeved button up shirt allowed his biceps to peek out just enough to make her glad to see him. She went over and sat on the chair across from him at the other end of the table, while hopelessly trying to ignore the woodsy fragrance that had been making her life miserable.

They were in their corners.

Richard looked over at Kayla. She was wearing an oversized T-shirt and some sweatpants. She smelled like berries. Her hair was wrapped in a scarf, but she was still stunning. She had tears in her eyes, visibly tired. He knew he had hurt her. What could he say? He was on the ropes.

"I am so sorry, Kayla," were his first words.

Silent tears made their way down her cheeks.

He wanted to wipe them away, but he continued, "I know I messed up. I didn't do it on purpose. I wasn't trying to play with you. I just got ahead of myself. Please forgive me."

She said nothing.

He continued, "These past weeks without you made me realize that I need you in my life. When I first saw you, I thought you were a very attractive person outside. Now, that I know you better I can see that you are even more beautiful inside. I know it sounds like a cliché, but that's the reality."

She said nothing.

He continued: "What you saw on Friday night meant nothing. I was only there to discuss business. Then, I found myself helping her carry drinks."

There was a break.

Kayla was ready to speak now. "It didn't seem like you were under duress," she jabbed.

"She asked for my help," he clinched.

"Did you have to accept?" Kayla sucked her teeth, highly annoyed at his explanation.

"What was I supposed to say, 'No! Ask someone else'?" Richard's palms were out begging for understanding.

Margo heard the storm from her room. "I hope those two don't kill each other out there," she said and shook her head, but had no intentions of exiting her safe haven. There was a boxing match out there and no opponent was a palooka. They each had to slug it out until they both decided to throw in the towel.

"And the man in the pinstripe suit with the ponytail."

"What man? Mark? Mark Cohen?"

"Yes, the man at the beach bar."

"What about him? I don't get it, Kayla."

"He was here, Richard! In my neighborhood, in my building, at my apartment door."

"What?! Why?"

"You tell me."

"I don't know, Kayla. I'm just as puzzled as you are."

"Well, Richard, he came to tell me that you were already seeing someone and he offered me money to stay away from you. That's why! I guess he was right."

"What! I had nothing to do with that, Kayla." Richard shook his head in disbelief. Mark Cohen had the nerve to go this far just to make sure that his daughter, Jennifer, got with Richard.

"Look, Richard. Be honest with yourself. What do you really want?" Kayla grilled. She meant for that question to be a blow.

"I want to be with you, Kayla," Richard pleaded for an opening from his fringe contender.

"So...you think that you can show up here with two bags of groceries and...'cause I'm so underprivileged that would be enough to sweep me off of my po' lil' feet? That tells me your true opinion of me," Kayla said, folding her arms tightly across her chest.

"It's not like that at all." Richard shook his head. "I came because I wanted to show you that I care for you and that I want to be with you." He pulled back pleading again.

"Or do you want to play around with the black girl from the projects in the meantime, but then marry the white girl who fits into your class?" Another blow! Kayla expected an admission at any moment.

"If I wanted to be with Jennifer, do you really think I would come here to see you?" Richard maintained his position against the ropes absorbing her blows. "I tried to communicate with you, Kayla. I sent you a text."

She stood up, furious. "One text saying 'Hey'? That's how much you really want to be with me, huh? You send one text and in two weeks you out there walking around in public with the chick you keep insisting is only 'a friend'." Kayla stood her ground.

She walked over to where he was sitting, looked him straight in the eye and continued:

"Richard, let me tell you something, I have had a lot of drama in my life. More than you could ever imagine. Being a twenty-four-year-old single mother of two was never my dream. I can't erase the past; and when I look at my kids, I don't want to. But I will make sure that the future doesn't repeat the past. I don't want any more Baby Daddies. I can't deal with anymore players whose plan is to use me to satisfy themselves or their egos and then leave me hanging, broken hearted with more mouths to feed."

He let her talk.

"Holding out until the right time is how I choose to protect myself. That day at your house really wasn't your fault. I don't know what I expected? I should have known better. I am actually more upset with myself than I am with you. I let my guard down and was moving too fast. For some reason, I thought I could trust you to show me a little more respect than I am used to getting."

She was finished. She sat back down in her seat. There was a break.

It was Richard's turn. He took a deep breath.

"Let me make something very clear. I don't feel sorry for you, and I definitely don't need to look for a black girl so that I can have a play thing. There are a whole lot of white girls who wouldn't mind that designation. I am not trying to buy your love with a few groceries. I could have handed you money if I wanted to do that." He continued, "Those bags over there in the kitchen are filled with groceries especially for someone who is recovering from fish poisoning."

Kayla didn't even know that Richard had his secretary call the kitchen to speak with Pedro in Spanish, hoping she could get some information out of him about Kayla's whereabouts.

He exhaled and said, "Look, Kayla, I don't want to fight. I just have one request...," he was ready to drop to his knees, "...can we please start over? I am willing to do it your way. I don't want to play games either. I want commitment too, and I want it with you." His voice, weary but very sincere.

They were poised toe-to-toe, and neither contender pulled any punches.

She looked into his eyes. This time she saw willingness. She smiled and wiped her tears.

He stood up and reached for her from across the table. He drew her close to him. "I missed you so much, Kayla."

"I missed you too, Richard."

The match was over.

"Do you mind having company for the rest of the afternoon?" he asked. In boxing terms, he was the clever stylist, using more skill and technique than power.

She smiled.

He took her smile as a *yes* and brought her over to the couch in the living room where SpongeBob was still on TV.

"Just one thing, though," he said, "do we have to watch this funny yellow dude all afternoon?"

She laughed. "So, what would you like to watch, Mr. Patterson?"

"ESPN," he said blushing.

"OK, but only for an hour. Then, we watch what I want."

"It's a deal!"

"Fine," Kayla said, relinquishing the remote control.

The two curled up on the couch and watched television for the rest of the afternoon.

Margo had, apparently, dozed off. When she caught herself, she pressed her ear to the door to her room and listened carefully for voices outside, but heard nothing. "Did they really kill each other out there?" she wondered. She cracked open the door, confirmed the all clear, and proceeded slowly down the short hallway. She looked at the dining table where she had left Richard sitting, but the chairs were empty. Then she saw the backs of their heads on the sofa. She smiled. They had gone the distance and both came out as champions.

CHAPTER 26

Clay was waiting in Richard's office bright and early Tuesday morning. He passed right by the pit bull at the front desk and stomped straight in, leaving the livid Marisol in his wake. Choice Spanish words, which Clay didn't care to understand, were still ringing in his ears as he made it to the doorway of Richard's office. It was empty, but he had no problem waiting. Richard walked into his office expecting to see Clay. He had already noticed Big T parked outside, and Marisol's face told the rest of the story.

"I need an update, brah," Clay said.

Richard shook his head. "I don't even know where to start," he groaned, resting his bag on the desk and gimping towards the window like a wounded boxer. He was still reeling.

"At the beginning." Clay was grinning from ear to ear.

Richard stared out the window. People were passing by, but all he could see was the scene that played out in his life the day before. "You saw me at the hospital yesterday, right?" Richard asked Clay. His eyes still fixed on the scenery outside. He continued, "Well, I went to see her at work, but she wasn't there. Turns out, she was sick from fish poisoning and couldn't go to work, so I went to see her at home. Man...it was wild!"

"You went to where she lives? And got out your truck?" Clay's eyes were wide open.

"Yes."

"How did you get into the apartment?" Clay tilted his head waiting for an answer. He was trying to imagine Richard standing at the door of an apartment in a government housing community trying to talk to a girl.

"I told them I was her boss," Richard said flashing a smile.

"And they believed you of course, because you're white." A broad smile appeared on Clay's face.

The two burst out in laughter.

"Yeah, I know," Richard gazed at Clay, "that's what I thought too. They even made an opening for me to pass through with the groceries."

"Groceries?" Clay's clenched fist was covering his opened mouth.

Richard enjoyed amusing his one-man audience. "Yes, just some things from the supermarket for her to eat. I bought whatever Google™ said."

"Google™?" Clay shrieked becoming more and more fascinated with Richard's tenacity.

"Yeh, Marisol googled what to eat when you get fish poisoning," Richard explained in detail.

"So what happened when she saw you?" This was precisely what Clay wanted to find out from the beginning of the story.

Richard filled his friend in on the details of Kayla's initial response. "She stormed out on me, man."

"This is so crazy, man. So, what happened after that?" Clay was totally amazed.

"Margo, that's her mom, went in to talk to her, and eventually she came out." Richard continued.

"You were getting nervous, huh?" Clay made fun of Richard.

"Nervous? I was sweating bullets, man!" Richard admitted. "I just kept forcing myself to stay calm, telling myself I had already made it that far. There was nothing else to do but to keep going and ride out the rest of the storm."

"So she forgave you?" Clay peered at Richard.

"Not without going the distance. Boy, it was a heated parring match...intense, I would say." Richard exhaled still tired from his adventure the day before.

"So, you were arguing too? Man, this is insane!" Clay was totally floored.

"I know, right?" Richard shook his head. "We both said what we wanted to say, though. In the end, we called a truce. Then we chilled for the rest of the afternoon together on the couch watching ESPN and Lifetime."

"ESPN? Nah, you deserve your props, Boss." Clay fell out of his chair and genuflected. Then, he started pacing around the office thinking out loud. "Let me see if I get this straight: You went to her job to look for her; you tricked her supervisor to give you information; you bought her food at the supermarket; you traveled all the way down West to find her; you maneuvered your way in the hood to get to her apartment; you survived power punches once you got in, and then after all of that you subjected her to ESPN." They bumped fists. "You the Man! This girl obviously means a lot to you."

"Yeh, she does, Clay. She does," Richard admitted with gleaming eyes.

"So, we're back on track again," Clay said like a proud boxer's manager.

"Man, and I hope it stays that way, because I'm winded," Richard said.

Richard's day just couldn't get started. He was limp. Yesterday's drama had sapped his energy, and he could hardly think straight. He had eyed the ceiling all night wondering what his next move with Kayla should be. He was white; she black. She grew up on a tiny island, in a government owned housing community all of her life. He was from the suburbs of Davenport, Iowa. He could handle all of those variables, but he couldn't ignore the fact that Kayla had two children. So, this really wasn't only about what the two of them could handle. He was truly at a loss.

Richard ambled out of his office over to his secretary's desk. She was organizing some documents for a new project that had just come on stream.

He thought about how Marisol had six kids for the man she had been with since her sixteenth birthday. She said she never regretted marrying him. Richard didn't know his real name, because Marisol only called him "Papi". While Papi had always called him Señor Richard. To Richard, Papi seemed to have been a mechanic from birth, because he was always so engrossed in repairing vehicles. Richard wondered if he had motor oil instead of blood flowing through his veins. Anyway, Papi and Marisol were totally committed to each other.

"Marisol," he said as he sat in one of the visitor chairs in the waiting area, "if you were a single mother and a man was interested in having a relationship with you, how would you want him to proceed?"

"With caution!" she said looking up at her boss.

Richard leaned in. "Why would you say that?"

"Boss, have you ever seen a hen with her chicks?" Marisol shook her head in the realization that Richard was probably never in a position to observe a chicken's daily life. He, after all, was not from the islands. Stray chickens running around freely was a regular part of island life—her life. Cars dodging a hen and her clutch of chicks were also sadly a part of island life.

"Protective?" Richard was puzzled. He couldn't see where Marisol was going with this, and he began to wonder if he would regret ever asking for her opinion.

"Fiercely!" Marisol cried. Then she continued, "Do you know that hens survive a predator attack 90 percent of the time. If you seriously want to be in a committed relationship with a mother, you have to seriously want to be committed to her kids. Children get hurt too."

Richard had to admit that the only thing he really knew about Kayla's children were their names, yet they meant the world to her.

Marisol went back to business. She handed Richard an unsealed envelope. "Don't forget the Golf Club charity." She knew Richard had already forgotten. "And check your email. You got a pool party and BBQ evite from Chad and Yvette Fenley. Let me know if you need me to reply to either of the two or both."

Richard had absolutely no time to check his emails and Marisol had absolutely no interest in his private life. They were the perfect match. "Slot the dates in my calendar for me please and give me several reminders. When is the BBQ, again?" He asked, sure that Marisol would know the answer.

"Next Saturday," Marisol said staring at her computer screen.

"RSVP - Accept, four," Richard instructed. Yvette was Crucian. *Who knows, Kayla might know her*, he thought.

As for the Golf Club Charity, which was a yearly event, the only thing Richard could remember about it was that it was after Clay's wedding. In four weeks.

Kayla was well enough to go to work the next day. Her mind and body were begging to get out of the house. She was sure that the fresh air would do her good, even though her head was still spinning from her ordeal the day before. She couldn't believe that Richard had come to visit her. He was the last visitor she would have ever expected. Where would they go from here? Her thoughts were all over the place as she whisked past the pavilion's office.

"Are you okay, Kayla," Ms. Bishop called out.

"Yes, I'm okay." Kayla said and kept going.

"Wait, Kayla." Ms. Bishop blocked Kayla on the sidewalk.

"Why this woman don't leave me alone," Kayla said under her breath. She was hoping to avoid any conversation with the manager this morning.

"I saw someone in a blue truck come by your apartment yesterday. And...he left kinda late. Your boss?" Ms. Bishop inquired with suspicion and moved aside.

Firstly, what was Ms. Bishop doing in the office this early? It wasn't even seven-thirty in the morning. And secondly, why was she interested in Kayla's visitors?

"Yes," Kayla said as she walked around the office manager and strutted away.

Ms. Bishop knew that Kayla wasn't telling the truth. "Remember no extra bodies in the apartment or the Government gon have to raise the rent," she shouted at Kayla.

Kayla knew that what she said to Ms. Bishop would be stored up for another conversation. She'd deal with it then. Right now, Kayla had a long journey ahead of her; and not just the road heading to the gas station to catch a bus. Kayla had to think long and hard about where her life was heading.

She stepped over the roots of the huge almond tree. The tree was full of greenish-white blossoms. The tasty fruit would appear soon enough. Suddenly, Kayla's destination seemed closer than usual. Her goals were finally within reach. Kayla's thoughts went back to where they were before Ms. Bishop interrupted her-- Richard.

She would be escorted to Richard by her mother, and they would both be in deep thought. At that moment, in the midst of this large gathering of family and friends, it would be as if they were alone together. So much had happened that could have prevented them from making it this far. Nonetheless, the reasons why they should be together helped them to overcome all of the obstacles. That day, they would vow to spend the rest of their lives together.

Was it wrong to dream now? She had jumped to the wrong conclusion about Richard. He was obviously ready for something serious with her, and there actually could be a future for them. She and Richard were like trade winds blowing from different hemispheres that finally converged, creating a surreal calm that she could never have envisaged. That was a relief, but deep inside Kayla sensed that there were still some hurdles to overcome. One of which was finding out from where she knew the man with the ponytail, Mark Cohen.

When Kayla walked into the cafeteria, Pedro approached her as she was putting on her apron and hairnet. "Did your Spanish friend get in touch with you?" he asked.

"Who?" Kayla asked. Then, she remembered that Richard had explained that the Spanish friend was really his secretary, Marisol. "Oh, yes. She did. Thank you." Kayla smiled at Pedro.

"Anytime girl," he said and shrugged.

Kayla suspected that Pedro was more than happy to be of assistance. Of course, he said nothing of the caller who came by to see her. Pedro was never the wiser.

That afternoon, Kayla had a meeting with Mrs. Merchant. It was a post probationary discussion which had been postponed several times for different reasons. But, it was finally about to happen.

"I am pleased with your progress, Kayla. Both at work and in the nursing course," Mrs. Merchant said. She continued with the standard questions. A meeting of this sort was scheduled to last for about 30 minutes. This particular meeting would be different, however.

As Mrs. Merchant wrapped up, she looked at Kayla and smiled. "I had a discussion with the course instructors about you."

"Me?" Kayla wasn't expecting that comment.

"Yes, we feel that you will be a good candidate for the Registered Nurse scholarship. It is offered to one student who has excelled in the LPN course." Mrs. Merchant observed Kayla's reaction to the news.

"But the course is still in progress." Kayla stared at her shoes. "I'm not sure what will happen as the material becomes more challenging." Kayla wasn't sure that was the response Mrs. Merchant was expecting. But she was definitely planning to keep her expectations low. Kayla couldn't handle any more disappointments.

"That's why I wanted to have this discussion with you. Nurse Ocampo expressed concern that your participation and general interest in the course had waned a little lately. Pedro also mentioned some of his concerns. We were wondering if you were having any personal problems that you may need help with?" Mrs. Merchant's eyes remained on Kayla.

"Huh?" Kayla gulped and looked up at her boss. She hadn't realize that her participation in the class had come under such scrutiny.

"We wanted to let you know about this scholarship opportunity so that you could focus and not lose out. So..." Mrs. Merchant bit the edge of the pen she was holding, "...are you sure that there is no issue that you can think of that I may be able to help you with?"

Kayla wanted to say, *Well, yes, as a matter of fact, there are a few things that you can help me with. Tell me how to be a single mother of two, work full-time and study for an intense course, while only having twenty-four hours in a day. You can also help me to figure out why I am in love with a man who understands nothing about the social circumstances I have had to live with all of my life, and who is, by the way, also white. Is there any way you can show me how not to lose my mind trying to figure out how all of this is going to work out? Oh, and one more thing, please explain to me why I can't stop myself from barreling down this bumpy road.*

There it was, hitting her like a ton of bricks. Kayla had just admitted it to herself. She was in love with Richard. "Nope, nothing that I can think of," Kayla said, shaking her head and looking straight at Mrs. Merchant.

"Great! We are expecting great things from you, Kayla. Keep up the good work." Mrs. Merchant tapped the pen against her lips and smiled at Kayla.

"I'll do my best to work harder, Mrs. Merchant," Kayla said, blinking tears away.

The meeting was officially over.

Kayla staggered out of Mrs. Merchant's office and headed straight into the restroom. She needed some time alone. Kayla placed her two hands on the vanity against the wall and inhaled.

Richard's phone beeped. One message. It was Kayla.

"Hey!" Her text said.

"Hi, how are you feeling?" Richard smiled at his phone.

"Better. At work today. Got the message that my Spanish friend called. No mention of you. Lol." She giggled as she typed.

"Lol," Richard imagined her face smiling and her fingers poking him.

"Do you want to come for lunch on Sunday?" It was an invitation. Richard had earned it. Offering food in the Caribbean is a sign of friendship and kindness. This man was being invited into a humble home to share a meal. It was the most her family could do to welcome him.

"You cooking or take out?" teased Richard.

"You'll see when you get there," Kayla replied smiling.

"I accept. What would you like for me to bring?" The Statesider in him kicked in with an offer to contribute to the meal.

"Nothing. Just bring yourself." Kayla typed knowing that Margo would be insulted if Richard showed up at the door with anything in his hands.

"Hey, next Saturday, a friend of mine is having a pool party and BBQ at his house. Would you like to come with the kids?"

"They would love that."

Richard could tell that including her children made her feel hopeful that this friendship might be going somewhere.

He was committed.

Richard had never dated anyone with children before. This was new for him. As a matter of fact, he had never dated anyone black. He also had never dated someone from the islands. Neither had he dated someone who was below the middle-income category. This was all totally new territory for him, but for some reason, he was all in.

At about eleven o'clock in the morning, Richard was ready to start working.

CHAPTER 27

Everyone in Kayla's household spent the whole day Saturday cleaning. Kayla concentrated on the living room; sweeping, mopping, and removing cobwebs from the ceiling and corners. The apartment would be subjected to all the things that constitute a good island scrubbing. Windows were washed, curtains were changed and chair throw covers were replaced. Kayla dusted every visible surface she could identify. Margo was in the kitchen preparing the meat for Sunday's lunch. The kitchen would be cleaned once Margo had finished with prepping.

Samaria and Adjoni focused on tidying up their room.

"I tired, Mommy," complained Adjoni.

"Why we cleaning so much, anyway. Who coming? Ain even December," Samaria chimed in.

"Go back in your room and clean under the bed too," Kayla said, shooing them back into their room.

Kayla would work on the bathroom tomorrow morning. Cleaning it the day before would be a waste of time since her kids had a way of always making a royal mess during bath time. Everyone understood clearly--the house had to sparkle for their visitor tomorrow.

Saturday was hectic, but Sunday was nerve-racking. Kayla woke up at five o'clock in the morning and met Margo already up and about. The meat had been slow cooking for hours. Kayla checked and re-checked every nook and cranny. Later on in the morning, she cleaned the bathroom and kitchen. When lunchtime rolled around, everyone was dressed and ready. They waited.

Kayla must have looked out of the window at least twenty times just to make sure. The last look revealed the blue Raptor™ driving into the parking lot. As Richard approached the steps, the lodgers warily permitted him to proceed, now probably fully aware of the reasons for his frequent visits to the area.

As Richard made his way up the steps through the crowd, his mind wandered on the day before. His Saturday was spent working on his renovation with Jamal. He tried to speak with Jamal some more about his family while being very careful not to pry. Ironically, the young man had opened up. Jamal had revealed things that had happened to him from the time he was a baby. Things that Richard, who was more than twice his age, had never experienced in his entire life. Every Saturday Jamal and other youths would go to the Center to wait for a stranger to show an interest in them. *How many kids lived like this around the world?* Richard wondered. *How do they help from losing their minds?*

It hit him that being part of the program at the Center was Jamal's way of trying to stay off "the steps". Richard's perception of the young man and his role as a mentor suddenly took on new meaning.

Kayla opened the door before Richard could knock.

"Hi, Richard," she said. "Welcome, again."

"Hi, Kayla. Thanks for inviting me--this time." He smiled. "Hi Margo," he said and went over to give her a hug. "Hi, Samaria. Hi, Adjoni." There were hi-fives.

Once Richard was completely inside, he noticed that the apartment looked different from the last time he'd been there. He could see that some improvements had been made. The space felt light and airy, sparkling. The curtains were now light blue lace with light blue satin valances. The covers for the chairs were floral with large blue flowers. The small well-worn wooden dining table was set with mix-matched dinnerware. The kitchen counter was full of food. There was a roast, two different kinds of pies, seasoned rice, salads, and drinks. Richard felt like the Governor of the Virgin Islands.

"You didn't have to go to all this trouble for me," Richard awkwardly told his hostesses feeling responsible for their hard work.

"It was no trouble really," Margo exhaled wiping the perspiration from her forehead with a hand towel that never left her shoulders while she was in the kitchen.

The food was out of this world. Richard had been to lots of restaurants on the island, but none of them could beat Margo's cooking. Kayla took credit for the pies, salads, and drinks. Richard enjoyed those too.

Over dinner, the conversation was all over the place.

"So tell us about your family, Richard," Margo asked.

Margo chose most of the topics. She hinted at wanting to know how Richard's family reacted to his friendship with Kayla--white engineer from Iowa dating black Crucian girl with two children from a government housing community. She wouldn't be surprised if they were totally against the whole thing. How much influence did his family have on him? What did his mother think? Richard smiled at all her questions. Frankly, he had yet to mention Kayla to any family member.

After dinner, Richard spent more time with Samaria and Adjoni than he did with Kayla. They were not allowed to turn on the television; instead, they played all the indoor games they could think of. Richard even introduced them to a few he had played with his siblings like the Listening Game and indoor bowling. Recently dusted photo albums emerged. Margo wanted to show Richard old photos of Kayla and Malik.

She really enjoyed telling stories about her two children. Richard could hear in her voice the pride she had in both of them. There was a lot of animation as she explained how she kept Malik off the steps.

"I pulled him by the ear and march him up to the apartment one evening when I came home from work and saw him hanging out on the steps with those guys," Margo said to Richard, recounting a situation with Mally.

Some of her methods would be regarded as excessive in Iowa, but in St. Croix they were quite normal. Richard did raise an eyebrow or two during the discussion. Strangely enough, he was pretty certain that Margo would do it all over again, unaffected by the barrage of information on modern child-rearing techniques. How else would a single mother raising a growing teenage boy command respect? Needless to say, Malik was now studying architecture in Massachusetts, totally grateful for his mother's strong hand.

Interestingly, Margo didn't speak much about Kayla as a teenager. It was kind of understood. The outgrowths of her teenage years were sitting right next to them on the sofa. In the last album were a few old pictures of Kenrick, their father, whom Kayla had so far never mentioned.

Richard enjoyed watching Kayla play with her kids. He could tell that they spent a lot of time together. It was obvious that the kids loved their mother very much. In their own small way, they understood the sacrifices she made for them.

He couldn't help but think about Adjoni in a few years. Would he be going to the Center like Jamal and the other young men hoping a stranger would mentor them? Adjoni's father spent all day outside on some steps as his son's life was passing by. How sad was that? The whole thing would seem so hopeless had it not been for his mother and grandmother who would give him all the support he needed to succeed as his uncle had.

At eight o'clock in the evening, in the middle of indoor bowling, Richard's truck alarm went off screaming and lit up the dim parking lot and surrounding area. He peeped through the window and saw some guys examining his Raptor's™ 4Po8 twenty-two inch black rims.

That was his cue to leave.

Kayla stood by the apartment door with her two children's arms wrapped around her legs. They wanted to make sure that Richard made it to his truck safely. Richard flew down the flight of stairs, waded past the guys on the steps who had again made a path for him, then trotted to his truck. After turning back briefly to wave goodbye, he drove off.

Kayla's phone beeped. One message. It was from Richard.

"Are you OK?" Richard expressed his usual concern.

Kayla read the message and smiled. "I'm fine. Thanks for coming," she sent back.

"Thanks for inviting me. I had a wonderful time. You have a beautiful family. Sorry had to leave so quickly.

Kayla looked out of her mother's window and saw the glow of his truck tail lights at the entrance.

"No problem. We had a nice time too." She typed and pressed send.

CHAPTER 28

It was the Saturday of the pool party and BBQ, and Samaria and Adjoni were beside themselves when Kayla finally announced where they were going. She chose not to say anything to them before it was time to get ready. Their excitement would have driven her crazy. Besides that, there would be no turning back and no excuses if plans had to change.

Kayla would have preferred to meet Richard at the gas station, but she had Samaria and Adjoni to consider. She was not about to make the long trek up the road with her kids. Besides, by now her neighbors must have been putting two and two together and drawing the right conclusions.

As Richard pulled up in his Raptor, Kayla and her children descended the staircase. They reached as far as the steps outside where they were held up for questioning. "Where you going?" Omari interrogated.

"Pool party and BBQ!" his kids blurted out, unable to contain their excitement.

"Your boss showing a lot of interest in you, Kayla," accused Omari, mocking a stateside accent.

"Wow! A busy father like you noticed?" Kayla shot back.

Richard grimly studied the exchange and squirmed in his truck. Should he get out to defend her? Witnessing the scene was unnerving. He opened the truck door.

Kayla looked up. She grabbed her kids, moved away from the steps, and marched towards the Raptor.

Omari gazed at the beautiful figure storming away from him. For the first time since their break-up, he felt a sense of loss and regret. Somehow he expected Kayla to always be around passing him back and forth on the step--admiring her from the back.

Kayla was a good girl. She was a catch. Everyone knew that.

He always knew that she was out of his league. Out of shame he had decided to move on to Tamara. Her expectations were much lower than Kayla's. It was clear that his kids' mother was moving on with her life now too. Omari watched as the liquid blue Raptor drove out of the parking lot with his heart. Just like Kayla's, his life was also about to change. All the boys on the step saw the somber and troubled look on their partner's face. They observed a moment of silence for Omari's loss. The act was over with this girl.

Heading to the pool party, Samaria and Adjoni were enjoying their ride in Richard's truck. This was the first time they had ever gotten a chance to ride in the cab of a truck. Who knew that some trucks had another place for kids to sit besides the open cab in the back outside? The giggles in the back seats made Kayla smile, yet there was a stillness in the front. Neither Richard nor Kayla said anything until he cleared his throat. She could feel the inquest brewing. Her eyes were fixed on the road in front of them.

Richard spoke once he thought the kids were not paying attention. "So what happened out there?" he asked.

Kayla had been hoping to avoid the conversation. It wasn't Richard's fight. Seeing Richard open the door of his truck had made her nervous. Omari was a coward, but not the other trigger happy guys on the steps. There was a reason he surrounded himself with thugs. Believe it or not, on those steps there was enough ammunition to start an armed conflict in St. Croix.

"Nothing really," Kayla said quietly.

"Nothing? Come on, Kayla. Do you think I couldn't tell? Was that him?" he nudged.

"Yes, asking about the amount of interest my boss was showing in me. Like it's his business." She frowned and sucked her teeth. How dare Omari act as if he owned her?

"So, what did you say?" The whole thing reminded Richard of Clay's words: "The drama is real." He wasn't lying.

"I told him that I didn't expect a busy father like him to notice," Kayla snarled, imagining the somber scarred face of her kids' father.

Richard looked at her and chuckled. "I guess you don't need me to defend you. You know how to handle yourself quite well." He reached for her delicate hand and tenderly held on to it for the rest of the ride.

It turned out, the Fenleys lived in the East End. Kayla shouldn't have been surprised.

Where else would Richard's friends live? It was typical, Kayla thought. Most whites on the island preferred to live far away from the locals.

The driveway was full of cars. As the four approached the house and walked through the opened double doors, Kayla saw a middle-aged, interracial couple standing close to the entry.

Richard initiated the introductions. "Yvette and Chad this is Kayla Jackson and her children Samaria and Adjoni. Kayla, this is Yvette and Chad Fenley."

"Nice to meet you," all three said in unison.

Kayla was surprised that the couple who owned this beautiful home was interracial. In fact, Yvette was Crucian, and she spoke her dialect as raw as ever. Richard never mentioned that to her. She did recall the night at the beach bar he had told her that he had Crucian friends.

"Welcome. Make yourself at home," Yvette said. "If you want somethin' to eat, we have food prepared." She pointed at the back beyond the glass sliding doors. The grill was smoking and the table right next to it was full of hamburgers, hotdogs, and barbecued chicken legs. "Or you could go straight into the pool. I know it looks full," she said looking over at the pool, "but we always ga room." She giggled.

Kayla gazed outside. There were more people than she had expected. She assumed that some were Yvette's family and friends and some were Chad's. The pool was full of kids and equipped with every water game possible. Some adults were sitting on the edge of the pool monitoring the children, but most were sitting at tables on the lawn--eating and drinking.

Samaria and Adjoni were expert party animals, thanks to their grandmother, and it didn't take much time for them to warm up to the other guests. Kayla had joined the group of adults that was cautiously watching the kids.

As the sun started to set, the crowd eventually dwindled down to the hosts and Richard's posse. The two families sat around the patio table on the deck. Understandably, the kids had a ball the entire time. But the chill in the air along with wrinkled palms had convinced the kids to come out of the pool and Kayla was relieved. They were finally ready to change into dry clothes. Yvette motioned to Kayla and she escorted them to a room where Kayla could tend to her children. Richard and Chad were left at the table glad for the quiet time.

"Hey, Rich. Kayla is Crucian. You didn't tell me."

"Sorry, I didn't think of mentioning it."

"I know. It doesn't matter. Two kids too."

"Yeh. I know."

"Well, it's all about what you can handle, right?"

Richard's mind was on the Charity. The Fenleys always got an invite. But he figured that there must be a reason why Chad didn't attend. *Did it have anything to do with Yvette? It probably had everything to do with her.*

He decided to begin his inquisition. "So...Chad, are you going to the Golf Club Charity this year? I don't remember seeing you there last year."

"Probably not," Chad answered quickly.

"Your dad...I mean Brad, never misses the event, though. He's there every year. I remember him dragging me along when I first started working with you guys." Richard was still fishing.

"Yes, you know how Dad is--unrelenting." Chad gazed at Richard and half-smiled.

"I already received my invitation...want to take Kayla with me." Richard waited for a response.

"Huh huh...interesting." Chad poured himself the last drop of lemonade that was in a plastic pitcher on the table. He gazed over at the pool and gawked at the mile-high pile of inflatable pool toys. "You know I will have to deflate and store all those toys for the next time Yvette has a longing to see a herd of kids wading in the water. "Where does she find this stuff?" he said and turned back to his guest, "Richard, let me ask you, how many blacks have you seen there the times you've attended?"

Richard was getting the message. He shifted his gaze to search Chad's face. "So that's why you don't go?" Richard felt a knot in his stomach. He could taste trouble.

"I don't want to make Yvette uncomfortable. We stay where we both feel accepted. She was my choice. I can't force anyone to accept her. They are free to make their choices too." Chad waited to see agreement in Richard's face.

"So Yvette is OK with that?" Richard needed to know what to expect from Kayla.

"Well, we tried it once, and I think it devastated her. Some of the same people we do business with every day, who are so polite to her outside, treated her as if she had a contagious disease when she walked into the club. Once she doesn't come into their circle she's fine." Chad didn't plan to hide the truth from Richard. His friend needed to know what to expect if he chose a certain path.

"So you don't think times have changed?" Richard sounded hopeful.

"Maybe, but we're not going to go through that again. You could try and let me know. You have to be prepared for what comes with relationships like ours, Richard. Everyone in the world is not as open-minded as we are."

Kayla felt Yvette eyeing her as she rounded up her kids. Although Yvette was Crucian, Kayla wasn't sure she could lower her guard just yet. She imagined that local people would be wondering why Richard wanted to be with her, just like the ponytail guy asked. They would be looking at her kids and trying to figure out her age.

"The last one, the bwoy, has to be five. So, how old was she when the girl was born?" she imagined they would think.

"This young lady can't be more than twenty-three/twenty-four," they would continue.

"How she and that white man meet anyway? Why was he even looking in her direction?" they would wonder.

"She a pretty girl," they would say. *"But who's she? Where she from? Who's her family?"*

"So, what he really want with her?" Kayla could hear some of them say, chuckling with insinuation.

There would be nothing about her being a bright young lady, a good mother who takes care of her kids, and a hard worker. She cut her eyes at the people in her thoughts. Not a word about her studying to be a nurse who might one day possibly take care of them if they ever became patients at the hospital. She sensed that Yvette was burning to ask her, "So, how did you and Richard meet?" But, she never did.

The ladies returned to the table hesitant about joining the discussion between the two men. They could sense that the conversation between the two men was a private one. Richard and Chad eventually excused themselves from the table and relocated to the kitchen. From there they had an unobstructed view of the pool and the deck. The house was designed beautifully.

Both men looked through the glass doors as they spoke, eyeing the two charming women they had chosen to be with.

"Richard, I need to get the kids home and in bed," Kayla eventually said.

"Did you guys have a good time?" Chad asked Samaria and Adjoni.

"Yes," they both said, drowsy with sleep.

"Come again, Kayla," Yvette said. "You're welcome here anytime."

"Yeh, don't wait for Richard," Chad said chuckling.

The four adults expressed how much they enjoyed the day and each other's company. Everyone promised to get together again. There was a sense of genuine comradery between the two couples, after all, they shared a few things in common.

The hum of the truck ride home quickly lulled to sleep the two exhausted children. Fortunately, the seat belts kept their tired little bodies strapped to the back seats.

"What's the charity about, Richard? Are you going?" Kayla gazed over at Richard as he concentrated on the road ahead. Yvette and Kayla had overheard Chad and Richard talking about a charity as they approached the deck. Kayla guessed that Yvette understood clearly what the charity was about, but she said nothing to Kayla.

"Something at the Golf Club," Richard said worriedly. He reached for Kayla's hand while he drove. He was honestly hoping they wouldn't have this discussion just yet.

"So, are you going?" Kayla asked, detecting the hesitation in Richard's voice.

"I don't know. I don't think I feel comfortable going this year," Richard admitted.

Kayla sensed that there was more to his answer. He seemed so guarded. "You mean you don't feel comfortable going with me?" She looked at him. Did Richard have the guts to take her into the "no-go zone" or was she reserved only for controlled environments like dimly lit beach bars, a pool party with an interracial couple, his house, her house?

There was a hush.

"It's complicated, Kayla," Richard moaned.

"What is so complicated, Richard? That there will be a lot of powerful, wealthy white people in the same room, and that showing up with me might not exactly help your reputation?" She wriggled her hand out of his grip. "Maybe we're not ready for this, Richard." Mally's words started beating in her head like a drum.

The silence returned, but this time it lasted for the rest of the trip. Richard helped her take the kids up to the apartment.

"Sorry, Kayla. It's not what you think," he said before she closed the door.

"Whatever, Richard."

"Good night hug?" He looked at her and smiled, hoping she was willing.

Kayla accepted. She would never admit it, but she desperately needed his warmth. She felt so secure in his arms.

"We'll work this out, Kayla," he whispered in her ears and kissed her on the forehead.

Richard weathered another night of deep thought staring up at the ceiling. This was becoming a regular occurrence. It seemed like every other day there was another challenge, another hurdle to overcome. Kayla's words rang in his ears: "Maybe we are not ready for this."

Maybe not.

The next day, Sunday, Richard's thoughts overtook him--Kayla and the Golf Club charity playing tug of war in his mind. Somehow, he had this funny feeling that the two didn't mix. He threw himself into his renovation to force his mind onto something else. It was futile. Was he being absolutely honest with himself? Was he ashamed of bringing her into his *world*, as she said? Was he ashamed of how he would be viewed? What would he do when his family came to visit? Hide her away for a few days? He hadn't even told them about Kayla.

Richard's phone beeped. It was Clay. One message. "Outside."

"Outside?!" Richard thought. "East End is a long way out to be in the neighborhood and just show up." He opened the front door to find a visibly upset Clay standing on his front porch. Richard signaled for him to come in.

"What's up?" Richard passed a cup of water in Clay's direction and sat on the stool next to his friend.

"It's Adrianna, man." Clay played with the water droplets on the outside of the glass.

"What happened?" Richard was looking at Clay, studying the agony written all over his friend's face.

"We had a big argument." Clay's eyes were fixed on the quartz countertop.

"About what?" Richard had never seen Clay so upset over a situation involving Adrianna.

"Something real stupid. Seating for the reception. We got real nasty." Clay rubbed his temples.

"Clay, just apologize. That's your girl, right. Nothing is worth losing her over." Richard counseled Clay. He would hate to see Clay and Adrianna break up over something so insignificant.

Clay looked at Richard and smiled. "You're a relationship expert now, huh." Clay looked up at Richard with hopeful eyes.

"You came to me." Richard smiled.

The two exploded in laughter.

"But you're right." Clay accepted Richard's advice. He excused himself to make a phone call to Adrianna. Richard heard him speaking to her softly, apologizing. He could tell that Clay's words were doing its magic. Clay returned with a smile on his face.

"You see!" Richard bumped Clay's fist, happy to be of help to his partner in distress.

"So what's up with Paradise Mart?" Clay exhaled, glad his ordeal was over and was eager to hear an update from Richard.

"Man..." Richard ran his fingers through his hair.

"Drama again? What now?" Clay prodded.

"It's that Golf Club charity thing." Richard looked down at the counter.

"The one I'm never invited to?" Clay chuckled.

"You know, I never noticed that before until now." Richard stared at Clay with apologetic eyes. The discrimination wasn't his fault, but he was willing to take the blame for the foolishness and apologize on behalf of his race.

"It's OK, because I wouldn't fit in anyway." Clay waved off Richard's attempt to soften the blow.

"Well, that's precisely what Chad said about Yvette." Richard ran his fingers through his hair again and exhaled.

"So, what happened? You want to take the Paradise Mart girl?" Clay raised a brow.

"Her name is Kayla, by the way. And yes...or...maybe. Actually, I'm not sure."

"Does she..., huh, Kayla, want to go?"

"She wants me to prove that I am not ashamed of her."

"Well, are you?" Clay gazed at Richard. If Richard was ashamed of Kayla, what would that say about the relationship that he had with Clay? Clay held his breath and waited for Richard's response.

Richard thought for a moment. "Umm..."

"That pause was too long, man."

"It's not that I'm ashamed. I'm trying to be cautious. I don't want to see her hurt."

Relieved at Richard's answer Clay said, "But, she isn't seeing it that way."

"I'm beginning to realize that." Richard rubbed his chin.

"Look, if you don't take her..."

"She'll say that I'm ashamed to be with her in front of other white people." Richard filled in the blanks.

"But if you take her..." Clay continued.

"She'll see that my feelings are real."

"Think about what's more important to you, Richard--what people think about you and her together or how both of you feel about each other. What is the worst they can do if you carry her anyway?" Clay patted Richard on his shoulder.

Richard looked at his comrade. He was so glad Clay showed up albeit for his own relationship issues. "Thanks, man, as usual. You know you're my best man if this thing works out?"

"It'll work out. You know that I'm there, brah. Just let me get myself married first. Look, I gotta run. I told Adrianna I was coming back." Clay got up and headed towards the door.

Richard would be Clay's best man in a few weeks. It was funny how they were both trying to help each other not to blow it with the women they loved.

After Clay left, Richard picked up his phone.

He typed "The charity event is two weeks after Clay's wedding. I'll send you the exact date and time on Monday. I would love for you to come with me. And don't forget Clay's wedding."

A few seconds passed. His phone beeped. One message. It was Kayla.

"Didn't forget Clay's wedding. How should I dress for the charity function?"

"Semi-formal, I guess. Something nice. You've never had a problem impressing me."

The dressing was the furthest thing from Richard's mind. He took a deep breath. Anticipating what that day would be like created bullets of sweat on his forehead.

Kayla read his last message and smiled. "I think everything will be fine," she typed.

CHAPTER 29

Preparing for Clay's wedding was exhausting--for Richard. He couldn't imagine how he would have been able to keep up with all the details. Clay, on the other hand, was enjoying every minute of managing another project. Richard knew his sidekick. This ordeal would be a piece of cake for that dude.

Richard could only imagine the planning that was going on behind the scenes. Clay had created a detailed checklist that Richard was meticulously trying to follow. Everyone in the company had received an invitation, even Marisol.

"Make sure you clearly specify the number of people expected to attend," Clay said to Adrianna who was busy stuffing envelopes.

"For the hundredth time, OK."

"That woman has six kids and a husband who is always covered in oil. Just imagine all eight walking in looking for seats."

Adrianna laughed, but she knew the drill. She was half Crucian, half Dominican from the Dominican Republic. Both sides of her family came out in their numbers to any event where there was free food. She carefully wrote in the number "two" on the RSVP card.

Mark Cohen's call to Richard broke up the wedding frenzy. "We are looking forward to your usual support at the charity in two weeks." The usual domineering roar came through loud and clear. There was no mention of Clay.

Richard now knew it wasn't an unintentional omission. "I'll be there, Mark." He said nothing of bringing a guest.

The day of the wedding was crazy. Richard had his dark blue tux hanging in his closet for at least a week. Clay had made sure that Richard wouldn't be running around at the last minute. He was always taking care of his boss. Everyone in the wedding party had to meet at Adrianna's house at a certain time. Then they would head to the hotel where they were all going to dress. Kayla didn't want to add more to Richard's plate. This was a big day for him too, so she told him that she would find her own way to the venue.

At the hotel, it was a mad dash. Hairstylists and makeup artists. Dresses, shirts, jackets, pants, and shoes. Flowers, corsages, and boutonnieres. Tons of last-minute details to decide on. A real madhouse. Then all at once, it was finally time for everyone to take their places.

Richard could tell that Clay was nervous. In fact, this was the first time he had ever seen his homie so ruffled. He went over to his sparring partner. Richard was so proud of him. He had come a long way. They had both grown together. Richard hugged Clay. "You got this, man." Richard patted Clay on the shoulder.

"Thanks, man," Clay said with tears in his eyes.

Everyone took their places. The venue was breathtaking. Adrianna had chosen blues, lavenders and purples as her theme. The wedding took place in one of the hotel's ballrooms. There were large glass windows that wrapped around the building inviting the tranquil view of the white sand beach outside to grace the ceremony as a spectacular backdrop.

The palm trees were swaying gently from side to side. Everything seemed as if in slow motion. The place was packed out with no less than three hundred people. No church could have held such a gathering. Richard didn't expect anything different from Clay and Adrianna. They both knew too many people.

Richard stood in front with Clay as the best man. He scanned the crowd for his girl, Kayla. *Did she have problems finding the place?* He would have loved to travel with her, but she insisted that she was going to find her way. Richard looked around several times at the hall that was already overflowing with anxious guests. Yet another glance at the entrance revealed a familiar figure slip through the large, elegantly carved wooden double doors.

There she was.

Kayla wasn't the bride, but for right now all eyes were on her. The color of her dress was cherry tomato. It was strapless and fitted. There was a beaded bodice and an ankle-length solid satin fitted bottom with an overlapping wrap in the front. A narrow rhinestone-studded belt united the two sections. When she walked, her strappy red heels peeked out with every step. Her hair was pulled back into a tamed, neat bun allowing nothing to compete with her beautiful face and striking red gown. She smiled at him, and Richard felt a warm sensation. The blood started rushing. "Don't embarrass yourself, boy. Calm down," he chanted silently to himself. Kayla found a seat and naughtily turned her gaze away from Richard.

The music began, and one-by-one the bridal party started to make their way down the wide center aisle. The bride anxiously waited to follow behind the procession. The room was slowly being saturated with hues of blue, purple and violet in dresses, bouquets of flowers, corsages, boutonnieres, eyeshadow, and lipstick colors. Gracefully, Adrianna appeared at the entrance.

She had everyone's attention.

How is it possible for an already very attractive woman to be transformed into an even more stunningly beautiful creature?

Clay was mesmerized.

Adrianna slowly glided toward Clay. There were tears rolling down their cheeks. Their journey leading to this point; the ups and downs, the ins and outs, all rushed through their thoughts. It was all so worth it. Eventually, the officiant guided Clay and Adrianna through the exchange of vows, and they became husband and wife.

It was a memorable event, and Richard was happy that so far the exceptionally large crowd was still under control. This was his first real island wedding, and he had a gut feeling that a show was in the offing.

A few precious moments were stolen to go over to where Kayla was standing. Richard hugged her tightly. He looked at her. She felt his affection even if he hadn't said a word. His eyes said everything.

"You look beautiful," he finally whispered.

Kayla wanted to have him stand by her side a little longer, but he had to leave to take the usual host of bridal shots. She could tell that he had come to mark his territory. His strong scent wrapped around her like a shield.

The wedding reception began eventually. All three hundred had been assigned seats. If anyone thought they could come to plop down wherever they chose, they didn't know Mr. Clay Barnes. Cleverly, Clay had set up the seating chart with Kayla sitting next to the bridal table with an empty seat reserved for Richard. He couldn't expect his love sick boss to endure the bridal table stage show for the whole night.

"Finally sitting here with my favorite girl. You okay?" Richard said to Kayla when all of the reception pomp and ceremony was over.

"I'm fine. I can see that this is your first time at an island wedding."

Richard chuckled. "Was it that obvious?"

"Yes, it was."

"There are so many formalities--the storm of speeches, some funny, some not so funny."

"You were fake smiling. I saw you, Richard."

"Come on, Kayla," he leaned in closer to her and spoke softly so that the rest of the table wouldn't hear his strong opinions. He knew he was outnumbered at this event. He continued whispering, moving his head closer to Kayla's, "How can you mess up 'Thinking Out Loud' by my boy Ed Sheeran? Seriously? Those were two unprofessional singers who insisted on serenading the couple they claim to adore so much. More love would have been shown by not singing."

"We are charitable, so we clapped heartily anyway, thanking them for their effort."

"Then, there was the dance group performance. It's exhausting. Is this what you want too?"

"Prepare yourself, baby."

Richard put his head in his hands. "Ugh."

"It's not that bad. The food and dancing make up for all of it."

"The food was incredible. I have to admit."

"I knew you would be impressed by the mile-long buffet table with every dish imaginable --from roast pork and Kallaloo to Johnny cakes and banana fritters."

"You know I love all of it. I got to hand it to the Crucians. You guys know how to throw down, and I'm always game." Richard was intrigued at the fusion of Dominican and Crucian flavors. The caterer had hit it out of the park. "I'm getting the best of both worlds," Clay had said to Richard when he explained why he had chosen Adrianna.

The DJ got his cue from the groom to start lighting up the dance floor. It opened up with the bride and groom dancing to "All of Me" by John Legend and then the crowd was invited to come on the dance floor. The Soca Electric Slide was the usual introductory anthem.

Kayla and Richard watched from their seats as close to three hundred people descended on the dance floor to take their spot in the lineup. The music was diverse. Juan Luis Guerra and Jam Band blended in seamlessly. Merengue, Reggae, Salsa, Soca, Bachata, and R & B. Every genre was on the line.

When Beres Hammond's "I Feel Good" blended in, Richard reached for Kayla. "Want to dance?"

"Sure." This time there was no hesitation. Kayla knew that Richard could handle himself on the dance floor. They stayed on the floor when "Pump Me Up" by Krosfyah started to blaze. The place lit up.

It was two o'clock in the morning when Richard and Kayla were ready to leave the partying crowd and head home.

The six-mile drive to Kayla's apartment was bittersweet for Richard. It was sweet that he had spent this special occasion with a lady that meant so much to him. For Richard, each moment with Kayla was priceless, and he could tell the feeling was mutual.

"Do we have to keep doing this?" he turned to Kayla and asked.

They had spent a wonderful evening together, but the night was coming to an end for them. His passions were all wrapped up in her straight jacket of rules. What was she afraid of?

"Doing what, baby?" Kayla asked.

"You know."

Kayla looked at his face. She sensed his agony. "Richard...I just can't. I'm afraid. It's hard to explain." She exhaled.

This was the bitter part. He couldn't take her home with him. "These are your rules, Kayla. I am doing my best to play by them." He gripped the steering wheel with both hands.

"I know," she whispered.

"Don't you trust me? I mean...I--I am trying so hard to understand your position, but some moments are harder than others." Tonight was turning out to be the former.

"One of the books I read said..."

"I don't care about no book, Kayla. We went through that already. Those books were written to protect women from players. I'm not a player. You know that. Don't you?"

"I know that now, but waiting just seems like the right thing to do."

"But why? If we love each other, why this torment? It just doesn't make sense to me."

Kayla knew that Richard was in no mood for quotes. Honestly, would they be rushing it at this point in their relationship? She had read so many books and gorged herself on interviews and talk shows. She even found scriptures in the Bible. All she wanted was to avoid the same feeling of emptiness that overcame her after every intimate encounter with Omari.

"Why buy the cow when you can get the milk for free?" her grandmother would say.

Was she a cow worth buying or should she always be giving herself away for free? If she gave in, would Richard see her as "free" or "priceless"?

"I don't know Richard. I'm just not comfortable enough right now. Sorry." She reached for his hand.

He pulled away. "Forgive me, Kayla; but right now, tonight, I just want you."

"I want you too, Richard."

"So then what's the big deal?" He looked over at her. "Why are you overthinking it? Love is so simple, so pure."

"It just doesn't feel right to me. Not now."

"All right, Kayla. I've already agreed to do it your way," Richard said, biting his upper lip.

Begrudgingly, he pulled up in front of the apartment building. He hopped out of his truck and went around to open the door for Kayla. He helped her down and kissed her. His eyes followed her as she meandered toward the littered, smoky steps. A path was respectfully made for her by the usual occupants who became speechless as she slowly made her way up in the sparkling, red beaded gown.

Kayla locked the front door and headed towards the bedrooms. Her phone beeped. Richard was checking in on her as usual. She imagined it would be a long ride home for him. But for once in her life, she was determined to be committed to herself, to her dreams, to her goals, to her choices.

Richard anticipated another heart-wrenching night staring up at the ceiling. "Kayla," he groaned as he clutched his pillow with all his might. He needed to know this woman, but forcing her to go against her instincts was not the answer. He had tried that before, and things went crazy. Although, at this point, he wasn't sure she would resist. Still, he wasn't going to chance it. Richard shut his eyes tightly and imagined the aroma of berries filling up his room.

This holding out *thing* was killing him. He cursed the stupid rules that people made up. He cursed all the celebrities with their theatrical talk shows trying to sell their point of view on *waiting* until the right time. Richard cursed the blabbing YouTubers™ on their homemade videos who now claimed to be relationship experts. The ones who after being promiscuous for years suddenly had a revelation that because they *waited,* their second marriages were somehow stronger. And he cursed the long-winded books that promoted all of the above. Richard wanted to curse the Bible too, but he knew that it was a holy book and he wasn't wanting to chance what the repercussions for that might be. He was almost certain that any damning words against that book would come at a price. Defeated, he pulled himself together and headed for the shower, knowing that the ice-cold water would do nothing to quench his thirst for Kayla.

CHAPTER 30

In the two weeks after Clay's wedding, there was no mention of the Golf Club charity--not in a conversation, not on a date, not even when Richard came over to visit Kayla at her home. Each had avoided the subject for different reasons. Richard, because he had already agreed to take her, so as far as he was concerned it was senseless to discuss it. *What would we be preparing for anyway?* he thought.

Kayla, on the other hand, had evaded the topic because she didn't want Richard to think she was a chicken and not up to the challenge. Although, she had thought about backing out a few times.

Kayla was patiently waiting in her apartment for Richard's truck to appear. The conversation on the ride home from Clay and Adrianna's wedding two weeks ago was still churning around in her head. She could feel her relationship with Richard approaching crossroads. He was tired of waiting. She could feel it. Maybe she was too. She had been staring out of the window for at least the past half an hour. Maybe it was her nerves. She had been on pins and needles for a few days now. Was it because this was her first charity event? She didn't even know what they were raising money for. Or was she afraid of another truck ride home?

The company this evening would be a well-dressed formidable force. She had never met these forces, but they had controlled so much of her life--her education, her employment, her livelihood, and even her healthcare.

When the blue Raptor™ finally pulled into the parking lot, Kayla opened her apartment door, flew down the staircase, waited for the path to appear on the steps, headed for Richard's truck and jumped in. She anticipated that the ride to the Golf Club would be long and mostly silent. Richard held her hand but concentrated on the road.

Kayla stared out of the window wondering how her journey had brought her here. She did want something more from life, but this was exhausting. Every few steps in her relationship with this man emerged a hurdle of some sort. Everyone expects positive results when they decide to take a chance. Neither she nor Richard, however, expected this to become a mammoth venture. She hoped that she would not be disappointed at the end.

Kayla looked over at Richard. "What's on your mind, Boo?"

"Huh?"

"What's on your mind? Why you so quiet?"

"Things."

"Do you still want to do this? Just let me know. If not, we can turn around. Do something else, you know."

"No, I'm fine, Kayla. I'm fine." Richard's eyes were fixed on the road ahead.

Kayla knew his thoughts were far away. Hers were too. They came to a long tree-lined byway. Along the way, there were a few openings in the bushes that revealed well-manicured landscapes that surrounded beautiful residences.

"So this is how the rich and famous live on a small island," Kayla said, sensing the Golf Club getting closer.

"Don't worry, Kayla. It's OK," Richard said.

They pulled up into the parking lot of the club. There was a parade of luxury vehicles, some of which Kayla could identify, thanks to her days on the steps when she was Omari's girl. Chilling with the guys on the steps brought her face to face with quite a few brave clients who dared to drive into the pavilion's parking lot in their expensive rides anxious to buy their choice of dope for the next high they craved. Besides that, "Bull Dog" always had a car magazine with him, and she would listen to him rave about the vehicles he dreamed about owning or redesigning.

Kayla saw a few Mercedes-Benz S-Classes, mostly in black. The Range Rovers, BMW 7 Series, Lexus LS, and Audi A8s were apparently the most popular ones, again, all mostly black. There were three Teslas and five Jaguars.

Richard parked his Raptor™ next to one of the Jags™ and came over to the passenger side to open the door for Kayla. She stepped out.

"How do I look?" she asked, suddenly feeling insignificant and poor--very poor.

Richard reached for her delicate but nervous hand and led it to meet his lips. He gently kissed it. "You look beautiful, baby. As always."

"And my hair?"

"It's perfect." Richard smiled. He squeezed Kayla's hand, and they began their stroll toward the glass doors of the Golf Club. All eyes in the foyer were already on them. He gripped her hand tighter.

"Don't feel like I belong here, Richard."

"You belong here with me, Kayla," he said.

As they got closer to the building, Kayla could see that the building was once a plantation great house. The year on the circa sign read 1774. She looked down at herself and smoothed out her dress with her free hand. She teased one curl with her fingers and started imagining the female slaves scurrying around the house, balancing baskets of food on their heads. They would be careful to do whatever their master had requested.

Kayla could see the slaves in their jackets worn with a petticoat and a full skirt. The linen or cotton skirt would be fitted at the waist and worn above the ankles to make it easier to move while working. *Was Caribbean history about to repeat itself?* Kayla glanced down at herself once more and frowned.

Mark Cohen was perched at the entrance. As territorial as a crow protecting its nest, he was ready to attack any intruder.

Donned in club captain regalia—dark green jacket with coat of arms emblazoned on the pocket and striped necktie embroidered with the Club's symbol, emphasizing his captainship--he greeted Richard. "We didn't expect you to bring a guest, Richard," he said, looking over at Kayla as he wiped the sweat from his brow.

The crow had spotted an intruder.

Kayla looked at Mark. That simple act of Mark wiping his brow brought back a faint memory. A look at the thinning salt and pepper hair pulled back into a ponytail jogged her memory a little more. Then, it hit her. She and Mark Cohen had a history that had started long before his visit to warn her about being with Richard. Mark wasn't only Richard's client, he was once Omari's client, too--a favorite, in fact. A client that Omari's uncle had turned over to him to get him into the business of drug dealing. Why hadn't she picked that up when he came looking for her that day?

He had caught Kayla off-guard. But now she remembered clearly. He told the guys to call him "Emcee". Of course, Emcee (MC-Mark Cohen). He had been coming to her neighborhood ever since she was in junior high school. He drove an old blue Toyota Corolla™ back then. He had a serious face, but he always smiled at her. Kayla knew that his smile was one inch away from being flirtatious. She was sure his self-control was only because he was afraid of the guys on the steps.

Yes, she remembered the ponytail. It was bushier then, more like a fox's tail. Now it was down to a fist full of strands twirled like a pigtail. Mark's hair was completely black at that time. His order was always the same, although Omari had tried over and over again to get him to try something different. A few drops or pinches of something extra and the price, as well as the addiction, would increase exponentially. All the same, Mark was a regular customer and the pay was consistent. Omari was pleased and didn't want to lose the business. Over the years, Kayla had lost interest in the transactions by the steps and hadn't paid much attention to the ebb and flow of clients.

That day when Kayla saw Mark at her door she wondered how he had found her. Now, she knew. She figured that he must have remembered her from those encounters on the steps.

When he saw me that night at the beach bar with Richard in Frederiksted, he knew exactly who I was, Kayla thought.

She clutched Richard's hand tighter. He hadn't visited the steps in years, but the guys would still know him. They probably gave him directions to her apartment. She wondered what lie he'd told them to get the information he needed.

"Hi, Mark," Richard said, choosing not to respond to the comment, but he managed to smile.

Kayla looked over at the sign in the Club's foyer. It read:

"Annual Golf Club Charity--Promoting Growth for the Underprivileged"

I guess this whole charity is about me.

The event was about to begin, and everyone started to make their way into the main auditorium. Richard led Kayla to some seats near the front. Kayla felt the stares and heard some whispers and snickers.

"This was a bad idea, Richard," Kayla said. She slumped her shoulders, wishing she could disappear.

"It's OK, Kayla." Richard's voice was low and resolute.

In no time, Mark appeared and whispered in Richard's ears, "Could you choose alternate seating in the back?"

"Why? Is something wrong?" Richard asked.

"Well, it's just that you and your guest may be a distraction to some of our paying members." Some in the audience sensed that Mark was giving the couple a hard time, and they didn't agree.

"Psssst. You guys can sit here," a nearby voice whispered.

"Thanks, but it's OK," Richard said.

"You understand, don't you, Rich?" Mark asked.

Richard stood up and looked around. All eyes were fixed on them. His thoughts started racing. First, to his Rasta friends in the hills who welcomed him with open arms as their brother. He thought about Clay who was his right hand in everything.

Richard could see Yvette Fenley in his mind, smiling at him. She was such a beautiful person, a dedicated wife, and a caring mother. He remembered Jamal, who was without a father or a mother but was still willing to take a chance on trusting a white stranger to help keep his mind focused on living and making something of himself. He recalled how Margo had invited him into her humble home and cooked a first-class meal for him.

Then, he looked at his beautiful Crucian empress, who at twenty-four had endured more than her fair share of trials, but who, in spite of many setbacks, was still pushing forward determined to give her children a future and a hope. Willingly, she had put her feelings aside tonight to support him. And at that point, he made a decision. If being part of this club meant that he would have to leave Kayla behind, then he didn't need to be here. If something was wrong with the black people who had touched his life in so many special ways, then he was sure that some of the people in front of him were not worth his time. He smiled at Kayla, took her hand, and gently pulled her close to him.

"No, I don't, Mark," Richard said and tenderly kissed Kayla's full lips. With that, he escorted Kayla out of the building.

That night he called his parents. He had something to tell them.

CHAPTER 31

Kayla's graduation was a few days away, and Richard had a special gift planned for her. Three days before the graduation while Kayla was at work, he met with Margo and the kids on the Frederiksted pier. They entered the gates to the pier and walked toward the old, red metal crane. The kids scurried over to look out at the water. Margo went to sit at a bench nearby, and Richard joined her.

Richard leaned forward, placing his elbows on each knee. He rubbed his hands together and said, "Margo, I--I would like to marry Kayla."

Margo's gaze was fixed on her grandchildren. They were still looking out at the sea, trying to spot fish and turtles.

Margo said nothing. Her eyes welled up and tears rolled down her cheeks. She wanted nothing but happiness for her children. She could see that Kayla was happy with Richard. She nodded "Yes". Richard put his arm around her.

When the children gave up looking for sea creatures, they joined their grandmother and Richard on the bench.

"I would like permission from both of you for something I want to do. OK?" Richard said to them.

Samaria and Adjoni both nodded as they looked into his eyes waiting to hear what he had to say.

"I would like to ask your mommy to marry me. I won't be your daddy, because you already have one. But I'll be your mommy's husband. That means that you will come to live with me, and I will take care of her and both of you until you are old enough to take care of yourselves. We will be a family," Richard said, trying to explain as best as he could to a seven and five-year-old.

"You mean like taking us fishing and playing ball?" Adjoni asked.

"Yes, like taking you fishing and playing ball," Richard confirmed.

Samaria and Adjoni's eyes opened wide. They smiled and looked at each other. "OK," they both said.

Margo's eyes welled up with tears again.

"Can you all keep a secret?" Richard asked.

They giggled and nodded.

Twelve months after her first day at work, Kayla walked up the steps to the platform where a panel was seated. Among them were

Mrs. Merchant, her face beaming with pride, Mr. McAllister, the Hospital Administrator, who managed to keep a smile on his face and Nurse Analyn. It was her graduation ceremony. The presenter had called her name.

"Kayla Jackson, recipient of the Registered Nurse Scholarship Award."

The day before graduation Mrs. Merchant had given Kayla a card. It read:

"Dear Kayla: When I first met you, I saw a smart, beautiful young lady whose spark for life was flickering. I could see that you were slowly giving up on yourself, but I decided to give you a chance. I dared to believe in you, and you did not disappoint me. Congratulations! Keep up the good work. Love Judy"

Kayla graciously accepted the honor. She looked out into the audience, but could only recognize a few faces. Her mother was giving her a standing ovation. This was the woman who had been her unfailing support--literally all of her life. Her kids were also standing next to their grandmother screaming and clapping cheerfully.

Then, her eyes locked with another pair. Someone all the way in the back against the wall. He was also clapping proudly. This was the man who had traveled a great distance making sure their worlds had converged. The road had been long and hard, with lots of peaks and valleys; but he was still here at her side. There had been so many obstacles to overcome; mostly in their own minds and hearts. Kayla was certain more challenges were still lurking around the corner, but this man had shown her that he was committed.

Once the graduation ceremony was finally over, there was lots of excitement in the auditorium. Kayla's mother and kids stormed her to get their hugs. Richard stood behind and waited for his turn.

"Congratulations, Kayla Jackson," he said.

"Thank you, Richard. Thanks for coming."

"I couldn't miss this, baby."

There were endless congratulatory hugs, proud family photos, and an infinite number of selfies with friends. After all the hoopla, the graduates eventually made their way outside.

Kayla's kids were walking at her side while Richard and Margo followed behind. Margo asked the kids to come with her to give Richard a chance to be with their mother alone.

Richard grasped Kayla's hand. "I have something to show you," he beamed. He cantered over to where his truck was parked but opened the door of the small midnight blue Suzuki Swift that was nearby. "This is my graduation gift to you," he told her.

Kayla gasped. "Is this for me?" She walked around the small sporty car, running her fingers along the shiny blue exterior. "Richard you didn't have to."

She had never gotten into the habit of taking gifts from men, not even from Richard. Her mother always said that when a man gives a woman a gift he always expects something else in return. Not that she would mind giving Richard anything he wanted at this point.

Kayla wanted to belong to Richard exclusively, but she wasn't in this relationship for financial gain. She was willing to work hard for what she wanted, and this graduation day proved that.

"I know you don't want any handouts from men," Richard noted as if reading her mind. He opened the glove compartment. In the glove compartment was a little black velvet box and a card. Richard continued, "But are you willing to accept a gift from your fiancé?"

He placed the box in her open palm.

Tears streamed down Kayla's cheeks as she nodded her approval. She wrapped her arms tightly around Richard's neck. He took that as a "Yes". Margo and the kids joined them as they kissed and hugged them both. They were saying "Yes" too.

That night Kayla's phone rang. It was her brother, Malik.

"Hey, lil' sis," he said, "I called to congratulate you on your graduation and on your engagement. I'm so happy for you."

"Thank you," Kayla said elated to hear his voice and to receive his approval.

"I warned you about this guy, but you didn't listen," Malik started, "...and frankly, I'm glad you didn't. You have always been one to take chances, and I admire that about you."

"I did listen to you, Mally," Kayla said. "Your words rang in my ears more than you will ever know, but I saw something in Richard that you didn't and couldn't see."

"Obviously. He seems like a nice guy. Mommy likes him a lot. And, you know, to get on Mommy's list..."

The two cracked up laughing.

"I was willing to take a chance with him, but I was determined not to risk more than I was willing to lose. I was not going to take a chance with my values ever again. Mommy fought very hard to instill them in us."

"Mommy really fought hard, Kayla. Even if we didn't listen sometimes."

"I wasn't willing to risk losing my dignity again. I've worked too hard to regain it. I was not willing to forfeit my future nor my kids' future for some frivolous, uncommitted relationship. A future which I was finally seeing clearly in front of me for the first time in a very long time. Your words made me stop and think many times."

"Kayla, I love you more than you know."

"You know I love you too Mally," she said. "But enough about me. What's up with you?

"Elena Benham and I are dating now," Mally revealed, "You taught me some lessons too. I'm learning not to be too afraid to take a chance."

"Congratulations!" Kayla screamed. "You gotta bring her to the wedding with you. I can't wait to see you. I look forward to having my mother and big brother walk me down the aisle in a few months."

The trade winds were picking up--making their usual rounds--as the holiday season was winding down. Kayla placed a small rectangular cardboard box on the wooden dining table and walked over to the rattling aluminum louvers. She grabbed the handle of the window and peeked through. Like usual, the sun was shining brightly on each building. The boys were on the steps as they were every day. They were arguing over something that probably made no sense, of that she was sure. She smiled. Her gaze landed on one particular person. She could only see the back of his head, but she could tell that he was making a serious point, and everyone decided to listen for a split second. Suddenly, there was a roar of differing opinions. The argument was by no means over. She shook her head, walked back over to the dining table and sat down.

Kayla looked at the box in front of her. Samaria's name was written on one side in eight-year-old handwriting. Kayla rested her chin on her clasped hands. She closed her eyes. Her mind wandered.

"Ready?" Richard's soft, deep voice whispered in Kayla's ears in the middle of dancing to "Beautiful in White" by Westlife.

She was ready, and very soon he would find out just how ready she was.

The ride home was silent; words were not needed. The only sounds were the whisper of the truck engine and Jah Cure's "Unconditional Love" softly coming through the speakers. Kayla rested her head against the truck window. There were buildings and cars and people and trees, lots of trees. Everything was flying by too quickly to focus on any one thing. Her life had been full of drama, just different actors, scenery, and props. The plot was constantly thickening. Curtains were up, and Kayla was center stage once more. Except, this time she was not alone. She looked over at Richard. Joy and contentment welled up in her heart. They both finally understood their plight and each experienced that moment of recognition as their story unraveled. Today was the moment of resolution. There was finally focus.

Kayla had promised herself months ago to stop dreaming. She found out the hard way that fantasizing about what could be, rarely ever turned out to be what actually happened. "Reflection is better," she often said to herself. There could be no doubts or mysteries about the past, she felt. It was already a done deal. For now, she let her memory continue the journey it was determined to take.

Richard held her delicate hand as he drove, enjoying the juicy scent of berries that took over his truck, his life, and his heart a few months ago. He was finally taking his wife home with him. At long last, after so many agonizing days, countless sleepless nights staring up at the ceiling and endless cold showers; she was coming home with him to stay. They had waited. She was resolute, and Richard complied. He had no choice.

Now, the wait was over.

They entered Richard's house. The place that would now become their home. The foyer walls and ceiling sparkled as the mellow and radiant moonlight filtered in, flirting with each piece of tile. It was exactly as her memory had captured it from the very first time she had visited.

Kayla looked around the apartment. It was spotless from the proper island cleaning that she, her mother, and her kids had put it through. She picked up the box and walked out, locking the apartment door behind her.

The trip down the stairwell felt longer than usual. As she stepped out of the building, Kayla took a deep breath and savored every smell she had become accustomed to--the mustiness of freshly cut grass; the medley of fragrances from each neighbor's laundry detergent and fabric softener; and the odor of stale urine on the wall, yet to be washed off by a good shower of rain.

She listened to the humming of dozens of washing machines mixed in with the cackling of Saturday morning cartoons. Kayla imagined children still in pajamas, sitting in their living rooms with eyes glued to the television. She could hear one of her neighbors in the distance playing "Cyan Mash Up Carnival" by Spectrum.

Kayla looked around at every scene that had been part of her world ever since she knew herself--the crowded steps ahead of her, the newly painted brown buildings.

Still dingy, she thought.

And Building 4 in the distance.

Every sensory experience etched in her memory forever.

She approached the steps with her box and there was a hush.

"Check you later, Kayla," Omari said.

"Yeh, see you, Omari."

"Congratulations."

"Thanks."

"Make sure you bring Sam and Adjoni to come check me."

"Don't worry, Omari, we know where to find you."

Kayla handed the box to Richard who was now standing beside her.

"Wha ayo saying?" Richard said to the guys on the steps.

"Yeh, man," they all said.

"See you," Kayla said and she walked with Richard to his truck.

They drove out of the parking lot and headed toward the exit of the pavilion. They passed the big mahogany tree and continued heading out of the community Kayla had known her entire life. She looked at the pavilion's sign and smiled.

Richard turned up the long road that she had walked up and down hundreds of times. She looked at the huge almond tree in the distance. There were almonds on the tree this time, and there was a crowd of children raiding the branches. She asked Richard to stop.

"Can you give me some almonds, please," Kayla asked, hoping the raiders were in a generous mood.

The children all looked down at their t-shirts that were used as sacks to hold the small purple fruit and then they looked up at Kayla warily.

Finally, one girl said, "Here, take mine."

"You going to give her all?" a boy asked.

"Yeh, you can't see she with her boss," the girl said.

"Well, he's my husband," Kayla said. "But thanks so much for sharing."

Kayla looked over at Richard and bit into the skin of the sweet fruit. "Mmmm. Finally!" she said out loud. "Not my boss, my husband."

Richard winked.

What the girl said made Kayla think about what had happened when their wedding announcement made it through the pipeline. Her family kept coming out of the woodwork, all determined to land an invitation. They were all so proud of Kayla, not only because she was getting married, but mostly because she was getting married to a white man. She had hit the jackpot as far as they were concerned, and they wouldn't miss this show for the world.

Richard's family, on the other hand, surprised him. He told Kayla that he didn't think that they would all make it. To his surprise, they all did--grandmother, parents and siblings. Kayla wasn't sure if they came to support him or to protect him, just in case.

Richard's grandma had tugged at his shirt and pulled him close. "Pretty girl," she whispered loud enough for Kayla to hear.

Richard's parents didn't say much, and his siblings seemed to secretly enjoy seeing their brother create a little excitement in the family. Aside from that, they probably wanted a vacation in St. Croix. Richard told her that this might be the first time his family would be around so many black people all at once.

"You nervous," she asked him.

"Not really," he said and looked at her. "OK, I would be lying if I say I'm not a little nervous."

The reception followed the usual island formula but was tweaked for Richard's sake. Clay told Richard not to worry about music, because that would be his gift. Richard's only request was that he include a few Oldie Goldie Rock and Roll songs for his family to enjoy. Richard's grandmother didn't seem to mind the diversity, though. She was on the dance floor with Kayla's uncle, Zach, who was showing her how to twerk to Soca music.

Granny was loving it.

The guest list included Richard's staff, the Fenleys, some of his Rasta friends, and Jamal. Clay did caution Richard to be more specific on Marisol's invitation.

Kayla's family did come out in their numbers, but no bouncer was needed. Margo invited Ms. Bishop, and Kayla invited some people from work. Mrs. Merchant was there with her husband. Shameka showed up with her baby daddy who although unemployed, was sporting an Italian suit and a pair of Air Yeezy 2 "Red October". Pedro escorted his mom, who came prepared with her own foil paper just in case there were extras.

Finally, Kayla wasn't dreaming. While Richard was waiting for the traffic light at the gas station, she reflected on how they had abandoned their party, leaving the crowd line dancing to "Hello" by Kes the Band. Their moment had arrived. Kayla couldn't forget how she felt the second they entered his house--their house--that night. Her mind played it over and over again.

She took Richard's sturdy, willing hand and led him in the direction of the wide, long hallway toward the master bedroom. As they passed the dimly lit kitchen, Richard pulled back and gently drew her near against his firm body.

"I can't wait any longer, Kayla," he whispered in her ear.

They had made it this far, and he told her that he was going no further.

Right there, they expressed the love that had finally been proven; the love that was undeniable and true; the love that, like the prevailing trade winds, had changed their lives forever and was blowing their hearts along a new path.

ABOUT THE AUTHOR

Wow! What an adventure it has been--from having the thought of this story and typing the first words to actually publishing my debut novel, *Trade Winds of the Heart.* I hope you've enjoyed the results. Thank you so much for journeying with me beyond the beaches, following Kayla and Richard as they were being blown on a turbulent path of twists and turns which lead them to self-realization and love.

Please feel free to leave a review with your thoughts. I would love to hear from you. Also, please visit me on my social media sites-- Facebook and Instagram.

https://www.facebook.com/KrystinaPowellsBooks
https://www.instagram.com/krystina_powells_books/

Krystina Powells is a West Indian American from St. Croix, U. S. Virgin Islands who has lived on or visited most of the islands in the Caribbean. The cultural nuances of life in the Caribbean make her appreciate that humor is found in the most unexpected places. She is a passionate author who playfully addresses issues that many shy away from while focusing on the often forgotten jewels of the sea which many call 'home'. Find out more about Krystina Powells at www.krystinapowells.com.